Prologue

He'd found her again.

The night creature's particles quivered in delight. His beloved! He'd been looking for his She-a for so long. Eagerly, his gaze drifted over the woman lying on the bed beneath him. She looked lovely, welcoming.

Just like home.

He hovered above her, so excited he could barely keep his amorphous form together. He couldn't wait to be one with her again. The energy he felt shimmering in her was so seductive, it made him ache. Waiting no longer, he lowered himself and eased into her from head to toe.

"Ahhhhh." Her energy, her power—he lapped it up like a cat drinking cream. He'd needed this. He'd needed *her*. "Why'd you try to hide from me, my lovely?"

They were so good together, a perfect match. They came together like no two ever had: she as his hostess, he as her guide. He hugged her arms around her and squeezed tight. He'd missed her so much.

Carefully, he coaxed her into a seated position. She slumped to the side but he propped her back up, bracing her hand against the mattress. The color of her fingernails immediately caught his attention.

"Hmm." He cocked her head, intrigued. They were a pretty rose color, just a shade lighter than blood . . . he experimentally scratched them over her legs. The stinging sensation made him cry out in delight.

Pushing back the covers, he did it again. Parallel lines of pink stung on her thighs, and he hummed with pleasure. The sensation was heady, divine.

Feeling powerful, he swung her legs over the side of the bed and stood. She swayed, but he balanced her and took a hesitant step. One step became two, then ten. Excitement filled him when they neared the top of the stairs.

How fun! Her last home hadn't had a staircase, unless you counted the three steps that led up to the trailer's door. He frowned, his excitement dimming. The last time they'd gone down those steps, they'd fallen. But he'd had to move her so quickly then. . . .

"We'll be careful," he promised.

She didn't respond—she never did—but they went down the steps together, one at a time. By the last step, the creature felt as if they were floating on air, dancing through clouds. Inhaling deeply, he waltzed his pretty girl into the kitchen. He could feel every beat of her heart, hear her blood rushing through her veins. Her power fed into him, strengthening him. Yet—

Suddenly, he sensed another presence. Hot, hard

In Her
Wildest
Dreams

attention bore through his hostess right down to him. It was blistering with hatred, bone cold with envy. Unable to leap out of her quickly, the creature spun toward the kitchen sink. "Dream Wreaker!" he hissed.

But there, framed by lacy curtains, wasn't his natural enemy. A figure stood outside the window in the backyard, peering inside. The shape was hidden, dressed all in black, but one thing was certain.

It was human.

The creature growled low and took a step forward. Those hot, hatred-filled eyes blinked in surprise.

The next moment, they were gone.

Outraged, the creature stomped toward the window and leaned She-a over the sink. The counter bit into her waist, but he was too angry to enjoy the sensation.

Why couldn't others let them be? Why must they interfere?

Pressing her nose against the glass, he looked outside.

Moonlight bathed the backyard, but he saw no figures lurking in the shadows. Still, he slapped the window with the palm of his beloved's hand. She was *his*. He'd just gotten her back!

The growl in her throat became a snarl. Turning on the ball of her foot, the creature surveyed her home. Windows, windows everywhere.

An eyebrow lifted when he saw the door to the basement. They could be together there and nobody would bother them. Yes. Down there in the dark, they could be alone.

*   *   *

It was cold, the kind of cold that worked its way deep into a person's bones . . . and woke them from a dead sleep.

Groggily, Shea reached for the covers but couldn't find them. Rolling onto her side, she wrapped her arms around herself and drew up her knees. They bumped into a soft, lumpy cushion. A warm cushion. Gratefully, she nuzzled closer. The well-worn fabric brushed the tip of her nose, and she settled back down.

Only something wouldn't let her sink back into slumber. Why was it so cold? It was summertime. But it was dark. It was always cold in the shadows.

Darkness.

With a sharp inhale, she jackknifed upward.

Where was she?

It was so dark, she couldn't see a foot in front of her. In that split second, she went from being half awake to being so alert it hurt. She *hated* the dark, and the pitch blackness surrounding her was the worst. Trying not to panic, she jerkily felt her surroundings.

She wasn't in her bedroom. There was no night-light glowing from her master bathroom. She wasn't even in a bed. That's why she hadn't been able to find the covers; there weren't any. Blindly, she traced the line of the cushions that had momentarily given her comfort.

"No," she whispered, her throat tight.

She was on a couch, but not the soft microfiber one

in her living room. She shuddered. The only other sofa she owned was the old one stored in the basement. The cold, dark, eerie basement.

Her feet hit the cement floor hard. Fighting her fear, she inched along, waving her arms overhead. Where was that damn light? She was breathing so fast her throat hurt from the dryness. She took another step forward, and something jabbed into the ball of her foot. With a hiss, she pulled back—only to let out a high-pitched yelp when something brushed her hair.

The light cord.

Spinning around, she batted at it with both hands until she got a good grip. One quick yank, and light flooded the room.

A whimper escaped as she stared wide-eyed at the shelves, boxes, and flower-patterned couch in front of her. She'd been right; she was in the basement of her condo.

Unnerved, she rubbed the goose bumps on her arms and double-checked all the corners. There were no monsters lurking; no intruders.

Except for herself.

"Please," she whispered. "Not again."

She'd thought she'd gotten past this.

Slowly, she glanced back to the staircase and followed the steps, one by one, upward. Dread filled her when she saw that the door at the top was closed tight.

"It can't be happening again."

Yet as much as the idea scared her, apparently it

was. For the one thing she knew for certain was that she hadn't started out the night here. When she'd fallen asleep, she'd been in her comfy queen-size bed, two floors up.

"God help me."

Her worst nightmare was back.

One

O neiros Intelligence Services. The name on the door greeted Shea as she stepped off the elevator. As always, a shiver of excitement ran through her veins. The warm rush was pleasurable, but the dull ache in her head wasn't. Neither was the tight band of tension around her chest. Nervously, she brushed her hand down her skirt.

Maybe she should have rescheduled. This meeting was important, but she wasn't feeling very well. After last night's . . . *incident* she hadn't been able to get back to sleep. She hadn't even tried. It had been all she could do just to keep the panic at bay. Even now, if she breathed too deeply, she'd touch upon that dark fear.

So she wasn't breathing deeply.

And she wasn't thinking about last night.

She was here to do her job, and was glad for the distraction. She always felt like she had to be on top of her game whenever she came here.

Or anywhere near Derek Oneiros, for that matter.

"Going down?"

The unexpected question made her flinch so hard, her briefcase bounced against her knee. "Excuse me?" she asked, turning on the heel of her white slingback.

A balding executive reached out and pushed the button for the elevator. "Are you heading down?" he repeated.

"Oh! No." Heat rose up into her face. "Thanks anyway."

Embarrassed, she stepped forward, gripped the handle under the stenciled sign, and determinedly pushed the heavy wooden door inward. Plush carpeting silenced her footsteps as she crossed the office suite to the receptionist's desk. "Good morning, Ellen."

"Good morning, Ms. Caldwell." The brunette rose from her chair and gestured to the office on her left. "Mr. Oneiros has been expecting you. Can I get you anything? Coffee? Tea?"

"Coffee would be wonderful." Anything with caffeine. Absently, Shea swept her hand along her cheek. At least the puffiness under her eyes seemed to have gone down. Now if only she could get her sluggish brain moving. "Cream with two sugars, please."

An infusion of glucose couldn't hurt, either.

"I'll bring it to you as soon as the pot is finished brewing," the receptionist replied. "Please, go right on in."

"Thank you." Tightening her grip on her briefcase, Shea turned toward the private office. She didn't know why she was so tense about this meeting; she worked with Derek all the time. He was the best at what he did.

Yet he also challenged her. The man was just an uncanny mixture of *GQ* and genius.

"Get it together," she whispered softly under her breath.

She couldn't let him see her so unsettled. If he saw for a moment that she was weak or off-kilter, he'd have questions . . . or he'd be concerned.

Her forehead rumpled. Now where had that thought come from?

Shaking her head, she gave a quick knock on the door. She'd just give him the assignment and leave. Her gray matter wasn't up to much more than that today.

"Come in."

The deep, smooth timbre of his voice was surprisingly calming. Some of the tightness inside her unkinked, and she took the deepest breath she'd managed all day. Letting it out slowly, she opened the door. He was already halfway across the room, coming to greet her.

"Shea," he said, holding out his hand.

Automatically, she caught it in a handshake. "Derek."

His hand swallowed hers, his tough skin brushing intimately against her softer flesh. Inwardly, Shea sighed in pleasure. She may have hired the man for his intelligence, but she wasn't a nun. His *GQ* appeal was why she always conducted their business in person.

Confused by the direction of her thoughts, she pulled her hand back. "I hope I'm not late."

He didn't answer. Instead, his thumb dragged across

the back of her fingers as if he didn't want to let her go. She looked up and found him staring at her.

A frown wrinkled his brow. "What's wrong?"

Her stomach took a dangerous dip, and her mouth went dry. So much for hiding anything from him.

Reaching out, he ran a fingertip along her temple. "Headache?"

She blinked when she felt her eyes unexpectedly sting. If only that was the extent of her problems. She felt panic start bubbling up, seeking escape and comfort, but she forced it back down. He was just being polite. "Do I look that bad?"

A derisive sound left the back of his throat. "As if you could."

He caught her by the elbow and directed her toward one of the chairs in front of his desk. "Sit down. Can I get you anything? Aspirin? A cold compress?"

Suddenly, sitting didn't sound like such a bad idea. Shea gratefully sank into the oversize leather chair. "I'm fine," she said as she set her briefcase on the floor beside her.

Her tension level shot back up, though, when she came upright and found him way too close. Instead of taking his own chair behind the desk, he'd settled his hips against the sturdy oak. His impeccable gray suit creased as he folded his arms across his chest and looked at her steadily. "Don't lie. I can see the pain in your eyes."

She licked her tongue across the back of her dry lips. She'd always found Derek an incredibly attractive man, but the way he was hovering over her made him seem bigger. Stronger. And with her emotions so close to the surface, all this fussing was making her downright . . . *aware*.

"It's not that bad," she insisted.

"I can pull the shades."

Her body heated as her thoughts went in a totally inappropriate direction.

"If it's too bright," he clarified.

The heat settled in her cheeks. What was wrong with her? "No need," she said, rubbing her palms against the smooth leather covering the arms of the chair. "Your receptionist is bringing me coffee. That should do the trick."

The lines on his forehead only deepened. "Caffeine withdrawal?"

Shea crossed her legs. On the job, Derek's tenacity was a distinct plus. Personally, though, it was disconcerting to be on the receiving end of that laserlike focus. "It was just a long night."

Silence fell upon the room and, too late, she realized the impression she must have given him. "Oh, no. Not that! I had trouble sleeping."

"Insomnia?" The question came out so quickly, he nearly spoke over her.

The reason for his concern became clear, and Shea suddenly wished the ground would open right up and swallow her. He didn't care whether or not she'd had a night of hot, never-ending sex. It was her lack of sleep. The entire city had recently endured an epidemic of sorts. For reasons unknown, people had gone through weeks without REM sleep. Unable to experience the recuperative power of the dream state, the victims had suffered terribly. And Derek's brother, Cael, had nearly been killed by a dream-deprived woman.

"It was just one bad night," she said.

She watched as his fingers wrapped around the beveled edge of the desk. One bad night or not, he *was* concerned. Impulsively, she reached out and laid her hand across the back of his white knuckles.

"I promise."

"Are you sure?"

"I'm fine, Derek." She gave his fingers a soft squeeze. "I've been dreaming. Lots and lots of dreams."

That seemed to settle him somewhat. He looked down to where she touched him. Even so, she was surprised when he turned his hand and caught her fingers between his thumb and palm. The contact sent a thrill through her. When she searched his eyes, though, his dark brown gaze looked haunted and uneasy.

"How is your brother?" she asked softly.

The question seemed to hang in midair. For a moment, Shea thought she'd crossed the line. As much as they'd worked together, she really didn't know Derek all that well. She had no right to be asking questions about his family, but he was worrying her.

A muscle ticked along his jaw. "He's better."

"Is he out of the hospital?"

"He's staying with his girlfriend." He looked down at her hand in his. With a soft touch, he aligned their palms more fully. "Cael's getting stir-crazy, though.

Devon's going to have a fight on her hands if she tries to keep him away from the newspaper much longer."

"That sounds good," Shea said, trying to find her voice. The way he was holding her hand was doing funny things inside her chest. "Isn't it?"

"Yeah," he said absently. "It's good."

"So why aren't you more relieved?"

He moved their hands to his thigh. It was the look he gave her, though, that stopped her inclination to squirm. One look, and she was pinned.

"Why couldn't you sleep?"

For a split second, she was thrown right back into last night. Into her basement, into the dark. Cold fear knotted her gut, and the panic collided with the breath in her throat. His hold on her hand tightened, pulling her back into the present. Into the daylight and into the professional workplace . . .

Shea slammed a lid on her emotions and smoothed her face. "It was just one of those things."

His dark eyes sparked. "Which one?"

She forced a smile onto her lips and gave a firm tug on her hand. "I'm happy to hear that your brother is doing so well. I know that your family has been through a lot."

"Shea," he said, refusing to let her go.

"Derek." She wasn't going to wrestle with him, but she wanted her hand back. *Now.* A knock on the door saved her, and she looked at him pointedly. "That must be my coffee."

*   *   *

Derek stared down at Shea. Something was wrong; he could see it. He could feel it.

"Mr. Oneiros?"

Hell.

"Come in, Ellen," he called. As much as he didn't want to, he dropped his client's hand. Pushing himself away from the desk, he circled it before his assistant could get ideas.

"Here's your coffee, Ms. Caldwell," Ellen said as she entered.

"Thank you," Shea replied.

Funny how he knew she wasn't referring to the hot drink.

The china tinkled as his receptionist placed the cup and saucer onto the desk. "Can I get either of you anything else?"

A few ideas entered Derek's mind, but he kept them to himself. "Thank you, Ellen. That will be all."

Leaning back against the filing cabinet, he watched Shea speculatively. That had been fear he'd seen in her eyes—raw, unfiltered fear.

The idea that she was having sleep problems bothered him a little too much.

He watched as she picked up the coffee cup. He knew he was staring, but that was inevitable. The woman was just . . . perfect. There was no other way to describe her. With that blond hair and tight, sleek body, she was gorgeous. That brain of hers was a major turn-on, too.

But something was different today.

He watched the way she held the delicate china as

if it were a lifeline. Her hands looked dainty and fine. When they shook and the cup tinkled against the saucer, he pinpointed the difference.

Today, she seemed vulnerable.

He raked a hand through his hair. He'd never seen her in anything but top form. What had happened last night?

"Ah, that tastes wonderful," she said, settling back into her chair.

He pushed himself away from the cabinet and made himself sit down, too. "I hope it helps."

She wanted to keep things between them businesslike, but sleep *was* his business. She didn't know it—and never would—but he had a vested interest in her dreams. *In everyone's dreams,* he quickly chastised himself. They were his family's domain; their responsibility and charge.

He and his brothers were the Oneiroi, modern-day Dream Wreakers. Descended from Greek gods, it was their job to bestow dreams upon sleeping humans. At night while others slept, his kind slipped into the dream realm to do their work.

Yet they'd failed recently, and failed miserably.

The incident with Cael and Devon had opened a door that should have remained closed. He and his brothers were still cleaning up the mess. But even the slimmest possibility that Shea was somehow feeling the repercussions made him ill.

Pushing her on the issue obviously wasn't going to work, though. "How are things at Biodermatics?" he asked.

"Very well, thank you. We're quite busy these days."

Busy enough that she was losing sleep?

"I see that you've landed Audrey Lowe as a spokesperson. That's quite the accomplishment."

"It doesn't hurt to have a celebrity endorse your skin care products. We're already seeing an increase in sales."

And obviously an increase in headaches. He didn't think she realized it when she reached up to rub her temple, but he did.

He let out a calming breath. Okay, maybe he was overreacting. He had a tendency to do that whenever she came around: *react*. One sleepless night didn't necessarily mean that something was wrong. A neighbor's dog could have yapped all night. Maybe the summer heat had bothered her.

Unfortunately, neither of those explanations accounted for the stiff set of her shoulders or the lines of tension around her mouth. That soft, pink, kissable mouth . . .

"How is the intelligence business?" she asked.

He flicked open the notepad in the center of his desk with his forefinger. "You really don't want to know."

Opening the top desk drawer, he pulled out a pen. His company specialized in corporate intelligence, data mining, and information security. These days, it was difficult to keep up with the hackers, white-collar criminals, and scam artists.

"You mentioned on the phone that you wanted a background check done," he said gruffly. "Are you hiring a new research scientist?"

"Actually, no." Putting her coffee aside, she reached for her briefcase.

The movement pulled at her white suit jacket, and his gaze fell on the vee neckline in a decidedly unbusinesslike manner. She was wearing one of those close-fitting, tailored suits that made a man wonder what lay underneath. A bra strap . . . something lacy . . . skin?

Skin.

His body started to hum. The tiny diamond pendant of her necklace swung to the side, though, and glinted at him in warning. Letting out a quick breath, he shifted in his chair.

"Phillip and I decided we need another secretary."

Phillip. Even with the warning, Derek wasn't prepared for the cold dash of water that was thrown over his libido. His pen poked a hole in the paper, and he grimaced. Ripping it off the tablet, he crumpled it and threw it in the trash.

"Tamika is great, but there's just too much work for one person," Shea continued as the latches on her briefcase popped open. "We really need someone to assist each of us."

Us. His hand fisted around his pen. Whatever had spooked her last night, good old Phil had certainly been there to take care of her.

The feel of her gaze on him made Derek tear his thoughts away from the unwanted visions in his head—visions of Shea and her too-good-looking partner. He looked at the manila folder in her hand and tried to think.

"A secretary," he said dubiously.

"Yes." She glanced up as she put her briefcase back on the floor. "Why?"

Saying nothing, he opened the file. The applicant's résumé sat on top, and he gave it a quick once-over. The facts entered his head on autopilot, for his mind was already churning over other things.

Like maybe he'd been onto something with his original work stress idea.

Tapping his finger on the corner of the file, he shot her a look. "Congratulations."

"Congratulations? For what?"

"You've made a breakthrough."

He had to give her credit. Other than a slight widening of her eyes, she didn't give anything away. It piqued his interest even more.

"Things are going a bit better with my research," she admitted, smoothing the edge of her skirt over her knee.

He watched her closely. She was always so careful when she talked about her work. Part of it was humility, but there was something else. . . . Sometimes he almost got the feeling she didn't want to jinx anything.

And he understood why. The implications of her research could be so far-reaching. . . .

Skin care products were Biodermatics's primary market, but Shea's personal efforts were focused on the medical dermatological market. Specifically, she was working toward better treatments for burn victims. Very few people knew that, and she paid him good money to keep it that way. Even under a confidentiality agreement, she'd only given him enough information to do his job.

Yet the pressure had to be there. The stress could be getting to her, and stress could do bad things to sleep patterns.

Derek leaned forward onto his elbows. "You've never had me do this thorough a background check for a low-level employee before."

"I think we need to change that."

"Okay," he said slowly. "I'll get on it."

A shy smile of thanks pulled at her lips, and he felt his cock harden. Oh, yeah. Major breakthrough. The woman was smart, classy, and devastatingly sexy.

No wonder she was taken.

Rubbing the back of his neck, he glanced down to the résumé. "So, Lynette Fromm," he read. "What do you think of her?"

Shea cleared her throat. "She seems bright and enthusiastic. She's called several times expressing interest in the position."

"But?"

She fingered her necklace. "But she's called several times expressing interest in the position."

He made a quick note. "Got it."

He skimmed through the information. "She has strong computer skills."

"And a degree in chemistry, so she should pick up on the technical lingo pretty quickly."

"There's a two-year break in her work history."

"She claimed she was taking care of an ill parent."

He flipped to the page of notes she'd taken. As expected, they were meticulous. "Her references seem to check out."

"But applicants always list people who will give them good recommendations. You taught me that."

He closed the file and set his pen atop it. Everything seemed straightforward enough—except she had his brain scattered all over the place.

"This shouldn't take long," he said. "Is there anything else you want me to check into?"

"That's it."

It wasn't much for the trip over here. "All right. Do you want me to call you with what I find, or should I drop by your offices?"

She blinked as if he'd surprised her. He became even more curious when she blushed.

"You can stop by the lab," she said after a moment. "That's where I'm spending most of my time these days."

He nodded. Whatever she was working on, it was big. He just wished she'd let him in a little more—on this and anything else she needed to share.

"How's the headache?" he asked softly.

Her lips parted in surprise. "Better."

Instinctively, his gaze dropped to her mouth. "Good; I'm glad."

He hated the idea of her hurting, especially if it had anything to do with sleep. "Shea, if there's ever anything else you need help with, you can always turn to me."

She hesitated. "That's very kind of you."

Kindness had nothing to do with it.

"It doesn't have to be work. You can trust me, whatever it is." He paused, suddenly unsure. "You know that, don't you?"

The air was suddenly charged with electricity, and she put down her coffee. She rubbed her hands together and reached for her briefcase. "Well, thank you," she said, uncrossing her legs. "I should get back to work."

He was on his feet before she could stand. "Why don't you go home for the rest of the day? Take it easy and get some rest?"

For some reason, her gaze went to his leather sofa—and, suddenly, that look of fear was back in her eyes. "No, I have a lot of things I need to do today."

Quickly, he rounded his desk. "Shea, what happened last night?"

"Nothing. I'm sorry I'm so out of it." She began walking backward to the door. "Thank you for your time, Derek."

He glanced toward the leather sofa that sat under the picture windows of his office and cold sliced through him. "Did Phillip do something? Did he upset you? Or . . . hurt you?"

"Phillip?" Her eyes widened, and she shook her head quickly. "Why would you think . . . Phillip would never hurt me. It was just . . . a nightmare."

Derek's hand curled around the back of the chair beside him, his fingertips straining the leather. Her explanation had the ring of truth to it, but that didn't make him any happier. As a Dream Wreaker, he knew that people needed nightmares occasionally to deal with their issues, but hers must have been bad.

Really bad. She was afraid to sleep.

She looked at the sofa again and paled. Showing less grace than normal, she turned on her heel and headed toward the door.

Something inside him wasn't ready to let her go. "I'll drop by as soon as I've got the information you need. And Shea?" he called as she caught the handle.

She paused and glanced over her shoulder. "Yes?"

"Sleep well tonight."

Her pretty blue eyes widened. "I . . . I will. I'm sure last night was a one-time thing."

No, *he* was the one who'd make sure of it. As soon as she was out the door, he was going to find out what had scared her so badly. He wouldn't feel right until he knew for sure.

"Have sweet dreams," he said firmly.

Her cheeks turned pink.

"Only sweet dreams."

Two

S weet dreams.

Shea's fingers slid absently up and down her breastbone as she stared at the bed. Just the sight of it had her conflicted. She didn't want to close her eyes. She didn't want to give up control—not after what had happened last night—but Derek had told her to have *sweet dreams*.

A warm rush went through her, and she inhaled deeply. Did he know what his words would do to her? Did he know what pictures they would put into her head? Her fingertips brushed against the swell of her breasts. Probably not.

Sighing, she rubbed her hands together to get rid of the remaining lotion. He'd just been concerned for her well-being. She'd seen it in the way he'd looked at her. She'd felt it in the way he'd held her hand. And to be honest, she was concerned for herself, too.

As scared as she was to put her head on that pillow, though, she had to do it. Being overly tired only made things worse.

Experience was a costly teacher.

Turning, she shut off the overhead light in the bathroom. She hadn't realized how dark it had gotten outside, and the momentary lack of vision startled her. Reflexively, she swatted at the night-light over the counter. The dim bulb illuminated the room gently, softening all the hard edges.

Softening the fear.

And softening her.

She hesitated when she saw herself in the bathroom mirror. The room was still steamy from her warm bath, and condensation gave her reflection an ethereal glow, a *sexual* glow. Her breath hitched as the moisture in the air made her nightie cling to her breasts and the tops of her thighs. The sensation sent her mind back to Derek, back to his soft words.

Her body shivered, her nipples perking up for attention. The sensation was so strong, she bit her lip. Her gaze locked with that of her reflection, and suddenly she wanted those dreams more than she feared anything else.

Before doubts could creep back in, she stepped into the bedroom. Her body humming, she lay down, pulled the covers over herself, and reached to set her radio alarm. It was then that she saw that one of the drawers in her dresser wasn't fully closed.

The sight made more than her skin cool.

"Damn," she whispered, unable to look away. As much as she wanted to believe it wouldn't happen again, ignorance was never bliss.

If that *thing* got hold of her again tonight . . .

The battle lasted all of ten seconds. Giving in, she scooted back to the edge of the bed. The slither of her silk nightie against the linen sheets sounded like defeat. Begrudgingly, she got up, crossed the room, and closed the drawer. Glancing around, she looked for other dangers.

The chair. She sighed. She hadn't had to do this since she was twelve years old, yet out of long-ingrained habit, she slid the potential obstacle under the vanity. She put her hairbrush in a drawer, and the wastebasket caught her attention next. She tucked it up against the wall.

Her teeth worried her lower lip as she looked across the room. She really shouldn't have to. . . . She walked over and locked her bedroom door anyway.

Letting out a calming breath, she evaluated the room one more time. The bedrail could cause a problem, and so could the sharp edges of the bedside table. There just wasn't anything she could do about them. Reaching up, she rubbed her shoulder.

Only sweet dreams.

She heard the words in her head just as the tension was starting to return. They sent warmth through her, calming her. She remembered the look in Derek's dark eyes, and her shoulders relaxed. If she just concentrated on him, how could she have anything else?

She returned to the bed, set the alarm, and turned off the bedside lamp. Letting her body relax, her mind went back to that comfortable chair in front of Derek's desk. The *physically* comfortable chair. Emotionally and sexually, she'd felt like she was on the hot seat. All that dark, brooding intensity of his was a bit overwhelming.

But fascinating, too, in all sorts of ways.

She tucked the sheet a little higher under her chin.

The man saw too much. Way too much. He'd picked up on her research breakthrough without her saying a word.

And her other secret!

She rolled onto her back, and her breath hitched. The covers rasped against her breasts, emphasizing the sensitivity in her nipples. When he'd asked if he should call or deliver the findings of his background check in person, she could have sworn he knew.

She pressed the back of her hand against her forehead.

Sweet dreams . . .

Why did he say that?

Sweet dreams . . .

He'd held her hand.

Sweet dreams . . .

"Come in."

Shea hesitated at the sound of the voice coming through the door. Surprisingly, the deep, smooth timbre was calming. Reassuring. Some of the tightness inside her unkinked, and she took the deepest breath she'd managed all day. Letting it out slowly, she opened the door. Derek was already halfway across the room, coming to greet her.

"Shea," he said, holding out his hand.

Automatically, she caught it in a handshake. "Derek."

His hand swallowed hers, his tough skin brushing intimately against her softer flesh. Inwardly, she sighed in pleasure. She loved meeting with this man; he was just so gorgeous. She took in his dark hair, handsome face, and mesmeric eyes—not to mention his rock-hard body. Surreptitiously, she let her gaze slide down.

If only he wasn't so ethical.

Confused by the direction of her thoughts, she pulled her hand back. "I hope I'm not late."

He didn't answer. Instead, his thumb dragged across the back of her fingers as if he didn't want to let her go. Time pulsed in that instant, and she slowly looked upward. She found him staring at her.

"What's wrong?" he asked softly.

Her stomach took a dangerous dip, and her nipples peaked hard. She hadn't had to say a word for him to notice she was hurting.

His intense gaze gentled. "Headache?"

She blinked when she felt her eyes unexpectedly sting. If only that was the extent of her problems. . . . But he was just being polite. Self-conscious, she lifted her hand to cup her cheek. "Do I look that bad?"

A derisive sound left the back of his throat. "As if you could. Come over here. Let me take care of you."

He caught her by the elbow and directed her across his office to the sofa that sat in front of the picture windows. She eyed the piece of furniture warily. Something about it made her uneasy. Yet the vantage point offered a breathtaking, high-level view of the city of Solstice. The sunny skies made the skyline look crisp and bright. Very, very bright.

"Sit down," Derek said. "Can I get you anything? Aspirin? Neck rub?"

She looked at him sharply. Her body heated, and her nipples perked up even harder. Stiff and achy, they strained against her prim business suit.

His observant gaze dropped, and his eyebrows lifted. "A neck rub it is."

His hands circled her waist, urging her down. For a moment, Shea resisted. His change in behavior confused her, but she was more than willing to go along with it. She'd just prefer the chair. She'd even lie down on the floor for him for a neck rub, but the sofa seemed wrong. Scary somehow.

"You can trust me," he whispered into her ear.

Her unsteady knees gave way, and she sank sideways onto the luxurious leather. It felt supple and warm under the sunshine—not frightening at all. "I'm fine," she said as she set her briefcase on the floor beside her. "Really."

"Don't lie." His lips were right against her ear as she sat back up. "I can see how much you need this."

A hot shiver ran through her. Instead of backing away, he'd settled onto the sofa beside her with one knee hooked up onto the seat. His shin pressed tight against her buttocks, and it was all Shea could do not to squirm. She'd always found Derek incredibly sexy, but this close he seemed bigger. Stronger. Still, she wished they were somewhere else.

"Maybe I'll move over here."

She shifted toward the oak coffee table, but his arm hooked around her waist. "I'll just pull the shades."

Her fingers bit into the cushions when he leaned across her and caught the drop cord. She could sense everything about him. His muscled arm brushing her shoulder . . . His hot breaths against her neck . . . With a flick of his fingers, he turned the blinds vertical, muting the harsh sunlight.

"Is that still too bright?" he asked.

If anything, it was too intimate and cozy.

Too dark.

Her nerves began to hum. "There's really no need for that," she said, leaning forward to open them back up. "Your receptionist is bringing me coffee. That should do the trick."

His hand wrapped around hers, stopping her. "Caffeine headache?"

"It was just a long night."

She straightened to nearly military attention when his hands settled on her shoulders. "Long how?"

Silence fell upon the room and, too late, she realized the impression she must have given him. "Oh, no. Not that." She twisted her head, and her nose nearly brushed against his. "I had trouble sleeping."

"Why?"

His voice was suddenly serious, his touch firm and protective. For a split second, it made her wonder if he knew of the dark creatures that roamed the night. . . .

But, no. He couldn't know. He was a smart, straightforward man. He wouldn't venture into the mythical world of children's horror stories that had ruled her life.

Still, his fingers were tense against her skin. One way or the other, he was concerned. Impulsively, she reached up and laid her hand across the back of his knuckles. She gave them a soft squeeze. "It was just a one-night thing, Derek. I promise."

"You can turn to me if you need help, Shea."

"I . . . I know."

"It doesn't have to be just business."

She melted a little. They'd crossed over the "just business" line practically the moment she'd walked in the door. Still, she wasn't used to this—not from him. Feeling shy, she faced forward.

Wordlessly, his fingers began moving. His thumb found a stubborn knot on the side of her neck, and her eyelids drooped. It felt good. The massage . . . Him being so close . . . Her body slackened, and she started to lean into the strength she felt behind her.

"That's better." His voice had dropped lower and so had his hands. His thumbs were exploring deeper and deeper under her collar, discovering sensitive spots. *"Just relax."*

Her suit jacket was in the way, so he tugged the collar down to get better access. The movement pulled the material tighter against her breasts, outlining their shape and form— and emphasizing the fact that her nipples were still as stiff as tent poles.

"Do you mind?" he asked, his hands suddenly sliding round to the three covered buttons that kept her jacket together . . . that kept her modesty intact.

Shea took a deep breath as she stared at his tough hands. Something far away told her that would be inappropriate, but she couldn't hear why. And what he was doing felt so right. . . .

"No, please," she found herself saying. She watched with intent fascination as he deftly undid the top button. Then the

second. And the last. Yet even loosened, the tailored fit of the garment kept it in place.

Her pulse began to pound when one of his hands disappeared inside. His palm settled onto her bare belly, and her muscles clenched. All of them. Her stomach, her thighs, her pussy . . .

His thumb brushed carefully against the bottom of her bra cup. "Do you know how long I've wondered what you wear under these sexy business suits?"

His mouth was against her ear, and his chest was pressed against her shoulders. A different kind of tension entered Shea when he caught the lapels of her jacket and began to peel if off of her.

She found herself helping, shrugging out of the confining material. Both his hands settled onto her stomach then. The contact was intimate and sexy. Slowly, his touch slid upward.

"You're tense everywhere," he chastised. Her back arched as his palms slid over her breasts, caressing the soft fabric of her bra.

She groaned and let her head drop back against his shoulder. She felt his gaze move over her. If she'd thought his brooding intensity had been overwhelming before, it didn't compare to how he looked at her naked. Her breaths quickened. Even so, she was surprised when his fingers glided across her chest to the front clasp of her bra. With a flick, it turned loose. Anticipation shot through her as the cups fell to the side.

On edge, she waited. When she glanced over her shoulder and searched Derek's eyes, though, his dark brown gaze looked haunted and uneasy.

He searched her gaze right back, but then his hands were on her, cupping her possessively, man to woman. Shea moaned in delight. The look he gave her, though, pinned her in his intimate embrace.

"What kept you up last night?"

The question threw her. "Excuse me?"

His hold tightened. "Why couldn't you sleep? Why are you afraid of this couch?"

Suddenly, everything changed. In a flash, his office disappeared, and Shea found herself in her locked basement. The light was dim, with only one weak bulb holding back the darkness. She was lying on her old, flower-patterned sofa, and she smelled something. . . . A hot, acrid odor hung in the air.

It was a terrible scent—one she'd smelled before.

Cold fear knotted her gut, and the panic bubbled up, choking her. Abruptly, though, she realized she wasn't alone. Soft breaths sounded behind her.

There was a presence in the basement with her.

"Oh, God," she moaned. It was here with her! She couldn't bear it. She couldn't look.

"Hey, now," a deep voice murmured into her ear. "Easy."

She twisted sharply. "Derek!"

He was there with her. Wrapping an arm about her waist, he pulled her onto his lap. His warmth hit her back, and his strength enveloped her. She could feel his arousal pressing against her bottom.

Terrified, she glanced about the room. The smell was seeping into her very pores. She could practically taste it. "You can't be here," she said, clutching at his wrist.

"I won't leave you." His fingers spread wide over her bare belly in a protective gesture. The fingers at her breast, though, began toying with her taut nipple. The clash of fear and desire was sharp. It caught Shea right where she was most vulnerable, deep between her legs. She pressed her thighs together tightly and caught at his muscled leg.

"We have to get out of here!"

"But how did we get here, Shea?"

"I . . . I don't know."

He bent his head. His hot breaths brushed against her neck, making goose bumps pop up on her skin. "I think you do."

She heard a sound. A crackle?

"No," she whispered. "It can't be happening again."

"What can't be happening again?"

"You have to leave. I don't want you hurt. Ah, Derek!"

The hand at her belly had become bolder, the fingers sliding far under the waistband of her skirt as the one at her breast toyed mercilessly.

"Tell me," he demanded. "Tell me what happened last night."

Her gaze flicked around the basement, trying to track the source of the smell. Where was the noise? It was getting louder, the popping and the hiss. "I thought I'd outgrown it."

"Outgrown what? You can trust me. I've got you."

"No," she said, shaking her head. "It's got me. It's found me again."

Her breath became choppy, her inhales too short. Her lungs ached as they struggled to get the oxygen they needed.

Her gaze went up the staircase, and she let out a cry when she finally found it. A flickering orange glow filled the space at the bottom of the door. Smoke was pouring in, and the crackle was coming from the wood itself.

Derek's embrace tightened, and he tucked her up against him more closely. "What's found you, Shea? What's gotten hold of you? Tell me."

Gotten hold of. Taken over. Assumed control.

Possessed her.

Oh, God. Fire! Fire! It had made her do it again!

Shea came awake with a jolt. Air rasped in her throat, her chest ached, and her entire body shook.

Jerkily, she reached out for her bedside lamp, nearly sending it to the floor. She grabbed it with both hands. Light, she needed more light!

Holding the lamp fiercely, she finally got the knob twisted. Light popped in her eyes, causing spots to appear in her vision, but she didn't care. She just needed to keep the shadows at bay.

Quickly, she searched the room. The space under the door was empty. No flames leapt. Smoke didn't unfurl. Her home was safe and silent, save for her harsh breaths and racing heart.

A nightmare. This time, it had truly just been a nightmare.

Shakily, she put the lamp back on the bedstand and made the conscious effort to calm herself. She forced her breaths to slow, but there wasn't much she could do about her heart. With a groan, she flung the covers off of her. Her legs were unsteady as she made her way to the bathroom, where she found her night-light glowing faithfully.

She turned on the faucet, but came to a dead halt when she glanced up at the mirror. Her eyes were wide and her skin was pale, but mixed with the lingering fear was something else entirely. Lifting her hand, she touched a strand of blond hair. It was tousled about her shoulders. And the blue in her eyes looked smoky.

She looked aroused.

Her cheeks turned a rosy red in the mirror. She *was* aroused.

"Oh, damn," she said, bracing her hands on the vanity.

Water rushed into the sink as she stared at her reflection. Now that the panic was tapering off, she could tune into other things—and her body was aflame. Her nipples were hard as little pebbles, and her belly was fluttering. Most telling, the crotch of her panties was wet.

"Oh, *damn*," she moaned.

Bending over, she splashed water onto her face. It was cold and bracing, but it did nothing to change the way she felt. Blindly, she reached out and grabbed the hand towel next to the sink. She buried her face in the soft terry cloth. She hadn't known it was possible to feel so good and so bad at the same time.

"Sweet dreams," she whispered.

More like hot dreams, *wet dreams*, with an all too familiar nightmare to cap it all off.

She turned off the faucet and tossed the towel back

onto the rack. Derek Oneiros. Derek Dream. She shook her head at the irony. She wondered if he knew the Greek origins of his name. "Oh, who am I kidding? The man knows everything."

Pinpricks hit the back of her neck as she stopped in the doorway and faced the bed. Her meeting with him today had been different—more intimate and distracting.

Obviously, he'd gotten under her skin.

And into her head.

Turning her back on the bed, she headed to the dresser. There was no way she was going to be able to fall asleep again, and sitting around here wasn't the answer. Not with the way her body was aching. . . . Not with the way her brain was standing on guard. . . .

There was only one place she could go and totally forget herself. One place where she always felt safe and in control.

Her lab.

Three

The room felt cool in the post-midnight hours. Cool and still, yet alive. Breaths wisped into quiet air. Hearts beat inside chests. Warm skin brushed against soft sheets. A breeze filtered in through the open windows as Derek stood looking down at the woman's bed. She was sound asleep, utterly relaxed with the covers thrown aside.

Then again, she always slept well. She was one of his best sleepers. She could sleep anytime and anywhere.

Tonight, it looked as if she'd had help.

He took a step closer and felt the heat that radiated from the entangled bodies. Sex still lingered in the air, but he didn't worry about waking the lovers. They couldn't see him, they couldn't hear him, and he wasn't here to harm them.

He was here in the dream realm, a parallel universe where only creatures of the night dwelt. It was here that Dream Wreakers' spirits could travel as they went from sleeper to sleeper, bestowing dreams.

The woman on the bed was his charge, a sleeper

assigned to his care. Right now her brain waves were calling to him, needing him to lead her into REM sleep.

He shook his head at the scene splayed out before him. This might be the only sleep she got tonight. "Let's get you dreaming before you're wakened for more."

This relationship was new and, honestly, surprising.

Yet he wasn't here to judge. He was here to do his duty.

Concentrating on the task at hand, he reached over the man's sleeping form and touched his charge's forehead. As if sensing him somehow, she murmured and lifted her hand palm up on the pillow next to her head. The gesture was open and trusting.

Derek brushed her hair back gently. A Dream Wreaker's power lay in his ability to manipulate brain waves, and through his fingertips he sensed large, slow delta waves. The woman was in stage three-four of the sleep cycle. Hormones were coursing through her body, restoring the breakdown that had occurred in her cells over the course of the day. He needed to switch that restoration work to her brain.

The man between them shifted, and Derek paused. He'd never seen him before, but the way the guy's hand curved around his charge's backside, he was sure he'd see him again soon.

When the man settled down, Derek tuned in more fully with his charge's brain wave patterns. He waited for the K-complexes to come, natural spikes in her brain waves that would signal she was ready to move into the dream state.

"There you go," he said, catching one of the spindles as they passed by.

Gently, he started to lead the woman up into REM sleep. Her breaths quickened along with her pulse rate. Her eyes began moving back and forth under her eyelids in the characteristic movement that gave the stage its name. The other muscles in her body went rigid as a natural protective mechanism.

"Good girl."

He waited for the movie to start to unfold in her head. He'd led her this far, but it was time for her to take over. Unlike some of his brothers who liked to play, he let his charges choose their own dreams. They needed to sort out their own fears and desires, not play puppet to his.

Although sometimes it was tempting. . . .

He finally let his gaze drift over the erotic scene. As far as assignments went, this one wasn't tough. His charge was an attractive woman. Short but curvy, pleasant without being cloying. Her blond hair spread across the pillow under her head, a bright contrast against the navy blue pillowcase, and his gaze stuck on the soft tresses.

Her hair was darker than Shea's, more like warm honey. Shea's was softer, sunlit. His charge's curves were more opulent than his client's. Shea's breasts were firmer, her waist trimmer, and her legs . . . He let out a long breath. She had great legs. Long, sleek legs that put dangerous, distracting thoughts into his head.

A tingle suddenly caught the back of his neck, and his concentration jerked back to the present.

Something else was entering the room, something non-human.

"Damn it," he hissed.

Leaving his hand cupped over the woman's brow, he turned, bracing himself. Dream Wreakers didn't seek out confrontation, but when their charges were threatened, they fought to protect them. And his charge was vulnerable right now as she slipped into the dream state.

A form appeared in front of him, faint at first, then becoming more solid and visible. Derek lifted his free hand and his muscles tensed, ready to do battle. The thing was big. Night creatures tended to avoid his kind, but when they were hungry enough, *needy enough,* they could be unpredictable.

Like this one obviously was.

"Whoa!" the thing said when it materialized. Only it wasn't an "it." It was a man who flinched and ducked when he realized another presence was in the room. "Ease up, Derek. It's me."

Derek rolled his eyes. "Don't sneak up on me like that, Tony!"

"Hey, I wasn't sneaking. Your head was somewhere else—probably for the first time in recorded history." His brother looked to the bed and his eyebrows shot up. "Now I see why. That's *hot.*"

"Is this your charge?" Derek asked, nodding toward the man in his way.

"No, but that one is."

Derek's jaw hardened as he looked across his charge to the third person occupying the bed. "That one" concerned him. Scarred and tattooed, he didn't look like the kind of man his charge would let inside her home, much less her bed. Yet the way the tough guy nuzzled his face into her hair and cupped her breast possessively told Derek he'd had her. Repeatedly.

"I don't like him," Derek decided.

"Ah, he's not that bad. He's an ultimate fighter, but he's got a good heart."

Derek slowly lifted his palm from his charge's forehead. She was dreaming feverishly—but not about the men. She was racing an Indy car going around the track faster and faster, out of control.

Tony grinned. "She must be a wild one."

Derek planted his hands on his hips. "She teaches first grade. This isn't like her."

"Oh, give her a break. Most people need to cut loose every now and then."

Derek's shoulders stiffened at the not-so-subtle jab. He knew his brothers considered him the unyielding one, The Machine, but he took his responsibilities seriously. Someone had to. In this case, his concerns had nothing to do with his charge's dreams or her sleep patterns. He didn't like the idea of her taking on more than she could handle. He didn't want her getting hurt.

She reminded him too much of Shea.

Not in terms of looks or even personality; it was the softness, the femininity, the vulnerability.

He glanced at the clock on the bedside table. Was she sleeping soundly tonight? Had whatever scared her been taken care of? He could practically taste the metallic bitterness of her fear, and it made his gut tighten.

Troubled, he glanced out the open window at the clear night sky. He could still go to her, could still check on her . . .

The knot in his gut twisted.

Or not.

He wasn't her Dream Wreaker.

Tony cleared his throat. "Uh, are you going to handle that other guy? He looks pretty wiped out."

Derek looked at the threesome, ready to be gone. But Tony was busy leading his charge into what was, no doubt, a bawdy dream, and it would be a waste of time for another Oneiros to visit the house. Impatience tugging at him, he slid his hand over the remaining sleeper's forehead.

Tony's eyebrows drew together. "What's up with you tonight? You seem preoccupied."

"Long day." Derek glanced again at his charge. He'd been trying to get hold of Zane ever since his morning meeting with Shea. His younger brother was the one responsible for her dreams, and he should know if she'd been having sleep problems.

Unless he was the source of them. . . .

Derek's fingers curled against the man's forehead. If there was anyone in the family more unlike him, it was Zane. Zane, the irresponsible slacker. Zane, the irrepressible flirt. If his brother had put some of his trademark erotic dreams in Shea's head, he'd have him by the throat.

Although she hadn't acted like her problem was erotic dreams. . . .

"Ah, hell," Tony said.

Derek's gaze flashed to the fighter and then up to his brother. "What is it? Is he not dreaming?"

Tony's attention was on the woman. "You look like you want to punch something. Do you have a thing for her?"

"For *her*? No!"

"Well, the way you were looking at her . . ." Tony's head snapped up. "Not her, but someone else?"

Derek rolled his shoulders. It had been worse than just a long day; it was becoming a very long night. "It's a work thing."

"I've never seen you get this knotted up over work." Tony's expression turned curious. "Did you get into it with someone? Because that's not like you."

"No, it's nothing like—" The man underneath Derek's touch suddenly dove into the dream state, and Derek was assailed by vivid pictures of him going down on his blond charge. Derek jerked his hand away, but it was too late. The real reason he couldn't go check in on Shea came into his head with startling, unsettling clarity.

He didn't want to see her that way with Phillip.

Yet even as he tried to push the pictures away, they kept coming at him. Shea easing into Phil's arms, snuggling against him, kissing him, climbing astride him . . .

Turning away from the bed, Derek raked a hand through his hair.

As much as he wanted to see her, as much as he needed to know she was sleeping better, he couldn't make himself go check on her. He didn't want to see them touching. He didn't want to see them sleeping side by side.

He didn't want to see her in bed with anybody else at all.

Tony moved away from his charge and slowly circled the bed. "Work thing, my ass. It *is* a woman."

A woman he couldn't have. Derek swiped a hand across his face. If Shea had been available, he'd have made his move a long time ago. But he wasn't one to break up a happy couple. From the very first, ever since he'd met her and felt the tug of attraction, he hadn't been able to get past her partner. The two seemed inseparable, together at all hours of the day. Phil had even answered the door at Shea's condo when Derek had gone to work on her home computer system. It was their familiarity with each other, though, that told how deep their relationship went. No coworkers he knew touched that way.

And the fact that Phillie-boy seemed to be a nice guy? Well, that just made it all the worse.

"Man, you never say anything!" Tony was standing right in front of him, reading every expression on his face. "You never talk. You're like the stoic king when it comes to this stuff."

You bet he was. His brothers could be worse than a church's knitting circle when it came to gossip, and he didn't want them talking about Shea. He didn't want them to know how he felt about her—especially if the feelings weren't returned. Just the idea of them feeling sorry for him had his skin tightening.

Tony didn't seem to get the message. "Who is it? Do I know her?"

"No." And as much as he wanted to, *he* didn't really know her, either. All he knew was that she was high-class, beautiful, and intelligent.

And his dick got hard whenever she walked in the room.

"Woo-eee," Tony said, rubbing his hands together. His voice dropped, but the smile remained on his face. "Come on, D-Man. This is good for you. You need something to shake up your nice, controlled little world. What's the lucky lady's name?"

"I told you, it's a business problem."

"A business problem that sashays when it walks. Hey, is it Ellen?"

"No, it's not Ellen!"

"But it is someone—"

"One of my clients may be having sleeping problems. That's it. Now let it go."

Tony grinned. "You first."

Derek let out a sound close to a growl. "I've got to get back to my rounds."

"You don't fool me, Machine." The grin turned into a full-fledged smile. "Going to see the mystery woman?"

"No," Derek snapped as he began to disperse. It was only through astral projection, the splitting of his spirit from his corporeal form, that he could visit all his charges. At the moment, he was happy to be able to disappear.

Because his brother was a little too close to the mark.

To the sound of Tony's laughter, Derek left the room and went off to find Tamika Hendricks. Shea's secretary *was* one of his charges. Sometimes, if he got really lucky, he was able to tap into her dreams to learn more about what was going on in the Biodermatics shop—or with her brainy, beautiful boss. Long-legged, sleek, and athletic, Tamika usually slept like a log. Lately, though, she'd been showing signs of insomnia. She'd been calling for him later and later.

After meeting with Shea this morning, the similarities had him concerned.

He hadn't heard Tamika calling for him yet tonight, and it was getting late. Honing in on her bedroom, Derek let himself manifest again. The moment he looked around the room, though, he knew he wouldn't be bestowing any dreams. Tamika wasn't sleeping.

Her bed was empty.

The night was heavy when the creature materialized in the room, hovering beside his beloved. Atom by atom, his form gathered, yet he had no mass. No substance. The fluorescent light from the overhead fixtures streamed right through him, and he looked at his faint shadow on the floor. All he saw was a shifting mist. She'd given him power last night, but he needed more.

Turning, he evaluated the room. This was a strange place to find her, so cold and impersonal. He was surrounded by stark machines, glassware, and computers—

yet she was here, his lovely. His molecules swirled as he drifted closer to her, itching to get to what he needed.

She sat on a high stool, her body slumped over the counter. Her arms were crossed on the countertop, nestling her cheek. Her hair spilled down her back, glistening in the artificial light. The brightness made him squint. He didn't like it when she fell asleep with the lights on.

He preferred moonlight. It was cooler, mysterious and intriguing.

Like her.

His pretty girl.

Reaching out, he stroked his clawlike hand over her soft hair. He growled deep in his throat when he couldn't feel it. In this form he couldn't touch, couldn't experience physical sensations.

That was why he needed her.

For the life force she gave him. For her abilities.

A sound outside caught his attention, and his head cocked to the side. He had to be careful; others could be about. But this room was quiet, except for her soft breaths. His nostrils flared as he sniffed the air to make sure. All he smelled was the lotion she put on at night.

It made his toes flutter.

He moved closer to her, aching and prickly all over. He couldn't stay away from her long, not in this state. The mist that formed his essence was already starting to dissipate and scatter.

"My She-a." He leaned down over her, his white mist

ebbing and flowing. He could feel her power, her energy. He breathed in deeply. "Mmmm . . ."

He looked at her eyes, and excitement buzzed within him. They were still. No dreams filled her head, so there was room for him. With a deep inhale, he hovered over her—and slowly let himself drop into her.

"Ahh," he sighed, feeling his power swell.

He opened his eyes—her eyes—and blinked. She couldn't see as well as he could. Yet he had seen something through her eyes last night, something she wouldn't have liked.

The memory of the window peeper flared in his head and he became angry. So angry, her body arched upright. He clenched her fingers around the tabletop edge. His She-a was *his* to watch. *His* to play with. *His* to—

He suddenly noticed how hard the bench was, how smooth and how cool.

Distracted, he ran her fingertips over it. Out of everything they experienced together during his visits, he liked the sense of touch best. He loved the textures, the tingles, the pressure, and the pain.

He licked her lips. Oh, the things they could do together now that they were both grown up. He unlooped her legs from the stool, letting her muscles do the work.

"Come, my pretty one," he said as he moved them clumsily around the room. He wasn't used to her size or weight yet. She was so much bigger than the last time they'd been together. She felt different: more capable, more sensitive, more developed . . .

More delicious.

Power hummed through his veins.

What could they do tonight? What trouble could they cause?

Items on the table suddenly caught his interest. Curious, he used her finger to nudge a beaker. Liquid sloshed. He saw another device sitting on the bench. He bent closer to it, and her blond hair slipped forward over her shoulders. It brushed against her face softly, tantalizingly. Reaching up, he fingered the soft strands and rubbed her face against them.

A scent drew his attention back to the strange equipment on the table. Her nostrils flared as he smelled something. He leaned closer, fingering the rubber tubing and running her nose against it. He could smell better than she could, and he inhaled the tart tang of gas. Using her finger, he traced the knob at the base of the device.

"Ahhhh," he gasped, lurching backward with her when a flame jumped.

Fire!

He hissed at it.

His She-a hated fire. It scared her. Yet he couldn't stop watching as the flame flickered and danced. Yellows, oranges, and reds. He started to sway with the colors. So pretty, so alive, so hot . . . He was reaching her hand toward it when the noise outside caught his attention again.

He whirled around with her, hissing louder until the sound became a screech.

There *was* someone out there. Infuriated, he closed her fingers into her fists. Why couldn't they leave them be? Why must they interfere?

The red from the flame filled his head.

Turning, he began moving her toward the door, gliding along as her steps became surer. He knew well the dangerous things that lurked in the dark. Mean, caustic things liked to hide in the shadows, but none of them were as dangerous or as mean as him.

Especially when his She-a was with him.

A crash filled the air, the sound loud and close.

Shea's eyes popped open, her muscles tensed, and her heart gave one big thud. Then it was off racing. Inhaling sharply, she looked around the room. Only she wasn't in a room this time.

The loud screech continued, making it hard to get her bearings. She was surrounded by an eerie green light, and numbers and a leather padded wheel. . . .

Oh dear Lord, she was looking at the dashboard of her car.

And it was running!

Her hands clamped down on the steering wheel. The rumble was loud and constant; she was dragging something! Her gaze jumped up to look out the front windshield. No, not dragging . . . pushing. She'd hit the Dumpster and was forcing it across the lot.

She jammed on the brakes and worriedly looked into the rearview mirror. Had she hit anything else? The streetlight at the far end of the parking lot looked small and distant, but she didn't see anything lying in her tracks.

That didn't make her feel much better.

To get here, she must have walked out to her car, put her key in the ignition, backed out from her spot, and driven two hundred feet.

The tension she'd fought all day came back hard, and her vision started to narrow. She breathed through her mouth and forced herself to focus on one thing at a time. The car was stopped. That was good. The green lights on her dashboard showed the speed at zero. The Dumpster rolled another foot or so before coming to a halt, and Shea stared at it, the accusing silence almost louder than the noise. It looked no worse for the wear, although she couldn't tell how well her car had fared.

A loud thud had her jerking again.

Her head snapped to the right and she let out a surprised scream.

Somebody was standing right beside her car, his gloved fists lying on her hood! The figure was dressed all in black, with the hood of its sweatshirt pulled over its head. The way the figure stood outside the headlights, the shadows nearly swallowed it.

But she saw it, and it looked like the angel of death.

When its head slowly swiveled her way, Shea couldn't contain her raw fear. Her hand flew to the gearshift, she threw the car into reverse, and hit the gas. Her tires screeched against the asphalt as she roared away from the person, stopping only when she was a safe distance back.

Breathing hard, she watched the figure through her front windshield. He stared right back at her, his face hidden in shadows.

Afraid to take her eyes off of him, she patted for her purse, looking for her cell phone.

It wasn't there.

Tearing her gaze away from the figure, she looked to the passenger seat. It was empty. A cold sweat broke out on her forehead. Where was her purse? She looked frantically to the building that housed her laboratory. Was it in her lab? Was that where she'd fallen asleep? She had her keys. Had she locked the door on her way out?

Oh, God. Her stomach lurched. She couldn't believe *it* had gotten to her there. Her equipment! Her *in vitro* tests! What damage was she going to find?

Her gaze snapped back to the black figure.

It was gone.

"Oh, no." Her throat clenching, Shea looked around the parking lot. She hit the locks, making sure they were activated, and twisted in her seat to scan the Solstice Industrial Park. Where had he gone?

What had *anybody* been doing here this time of night?

"Think!"

She wanted to check her lab to make sure everything was all right. Her research was so important—but so was her safety. She hated leaving all that confidential information exposed and maybe ruined, but she wasn't getting out of her car for anything.

Shakily, she put the car into drive and headed for the

exit. She had to get help. She couldn't make this situation right by herself. For a moment, she thought about calling Derek.

"No—Phillip." He'd know what to look for in the lab, and she wouldn't have to face that piercing, questioning look. Questioning why she'd left her purse behind, why she'd left her experiments half finished, why she'd left the building unlocked, how she'd found herself in her car . . .

Shea stepped harder on the gas. She knew the answer to those questions, and it was her worst fear come to life. Finding herself in her basement the other night hadn't been a fluke. She was sleepwalking again. She was sleep *driving!*

Her Somnambulist was back—and back with a vengeance.

Four

"What happened?" Derek demanded as he strode into Shea's lab. In the dark pre-dawn hour, the question came out too loud and too worried, but he couldn't take it back—even if he wanted to.

She was sitting on a high stool next to her lab bench, absorbed in her work. She glanced at him distractedly, then did a double take. "Derek? What are you doing here?"

She couldn't be serious. "Phil called. He said you might have had a security breach."

"I told him nothing was missing. I thought you'd just check to see if our computer firewalls had been breached or something."

Derek's eyes narrowed. She knew better than that.

"Just because nothing is missing doesn't mean somebody didn't get in here and poke around." He let his gaze rake over her. She looked okay, physically. That had been his primary concern as he'd raced across town. "Why didn't you call me?"

Her gaze swiveled away to the lab book lying open beside the microscope. Purposefully, she began writing notes. "Phillip did—and I contacted Industrial Park Security. They just left."

That wasn't what he'd meant.

His fingers curled around the back of an empty stool. She'd been alone, and it had been so late at night. She didn't know what lurked out there in the darkness. He did. "I need to know what happened—all of it."

She sighed. "What exactly did Phillip tell you?"

Derek reached up to rub the back of his neck. "He said you encountered a prowler in the parking lot. That was pretty much it."

"That *was* pretty much it." Her fingers tightened around her pencil. "He gave me quite a start, though."

"Why were you even here?"

"I came in to run a few more tests."

"They couldn't wait until this morning?"

"I couldn't sleep."

"Again?" He took a step toward her.

She met his gaze impatiently. "I had another nightmare. Please don't push this, Derek."

He planted his hand on his hip. Nightmares two nights in a row was beyond normal. What issue had her so wound up? Had she had suspicions before tonight that someone was trying to steal her ideas? Was that the source of the fear he'd seen at their meeting? "What was it about?"

She flushed. "Nothing."

"Try again."

Her cheeks turned even brighter. "I don't remember."

The electricity between them suddenly returned, the heat and the awareness. She remembered, all right, yet her reaction made no sense—until Derek remembered who gave her those dreams. His jaw tightened. If Zane had tried to give her an erotic dream that she didn't want . . .

Shea turned off her microscope, extinguishing its light, and recorded additional notes in her lab book. Derek took the hint. She might not want to talk about it, but he and Zane were going to have a close, personal chat soon.

Right now Shea had him concerned. A prowler was nothing to take lightly, yet it almost seemed as if she didn't want him here—and that stung.

Well, want him or not, it was his job to make sure she and her work were safe. "What time did you come in?" he asked.

"Around one o'clock."

"When did you first notice something was wrong? Did he try to get into the building?"

She ran a hand through her hair. "I don't know. I tend not to notice things around me when I'm working. It wasn't until I was in my car that I saw him."

"So you were leaving? But Phil said the building was left unlocked; that's why he called me."

Her fingers paused in the process of screwing the top back onto an open petri dish. "Like I said, I can get pretty engrossed."

He watched as she stowed the petri dish in its rightful place, lining it up with similar ones and making sure the label showed clearly. "Right," he said. "So that's why the Bunsen burner was left on, too."

Her gaze flashed to the burn unit and the color that had pinkened her cheeks drained out. Nervously, she licked her lips. "I did that."

"Shea, you wouldn't—"

"I did."

She stood abruptly, closing her lab book with a snap. Turning away, she pulled the glass slide out from under the microscope's objective lens. She disposed of it in a sharps container, walked past the fume hood that took up most of the side wall, and turned on the faucet over the sink.

Derek watched her closely as she washed her hands. She was no absentminded professor. Her movements were confident and precise; everything in her private lab was clean and tidy. This was her world, her domain. In here, she was in control.

But last night, all that had been threatened.

"You must have left in a hurry," he said gently.

She wiped her hands and tossed the paper towel in the trash. "I honestly don't remember."

He looked around the lab again, taking in the details. This place was her escape, her inner sanctum—and it showed little parts of her he hadn't noticed before.

Her mechanical pencil was hot pink, which surprised him. Soft rock poured from the radio atop a file cabinet, and a Mets calendar hung on the far wall.

"What?" she asked.

He met her look in the eye. "I've never seen you work before—not in your scientific capacity. It's like watching Einstein in his natural environment."

She blinked. "Einstein was a theoretical physicist, and a man."

"Then Madame Curie."

Her lips parted in surprise. "She studied radiation."

"Take the compliment, Shea."

They stared at each other for a long, quiet moment. "Thank you," she whispered.

Derek wanted to pull her into his arms so badly he could barely stand it—but it wasn't the right time or the right place.

"So when you and Phillip came back, nothing was missing," he said gruffly. He gestured about the room. "Was anything out of place?"

Her gaze locked on the Bunsen burner and almost compulsively, she reached past him to check that it was fully off.

"Except for that, no." Moving stiffly, she turned and headed for the door. "I was in my car when I noticed the person outside. I'll show you where I saw him."

Derek glanced at the burner. It made him almost as uneasy as it made her. He couldn't imagine that a competitor would try to burn her out. Not only was it extreme, it ran directly against the work that everyone in her field was trying to do. Yet he couldn't see her accidentally leaving it on, either—unless she'd been frightened.

Turning on his heel, he went to catch up with her.

She was just opening the door to the front staging room when he turned into the hallway. He found her there, reaching to take off her lab coat.

"Here, let me," he said, stepping up to help her.

She hesitated as his hands went around to the lapels of the white jacket. The move put him close to her, so close her scent wafted around him. Her hair swept over his hand, and his fingers stiffened on the cotton material. He wanted to be touching her skin.

"Are you sure you're okay?" he asked quietly.

For a split second, he sensed her leaning back toward him. Then the moment was gone.

"I'm fine."

He wasn't so sure. He could feel the energy rumbling inside her: the nerves, the questions, the awareness. . . . Goose bumps had popped up on the back of her neck.

Trying to keep his touch easy and platonic, he pulled the lab coat off her shoulders and down her arms. Even so, he couldn't stop his fingers from lingering as they brushed against her hands. "Next time you call me," he said, his voice rough.

She inhaled softly, but didn't respond.

He put her lab coat on a hanger and noticed her hands weren't steady as she retrieved her lab book from the counter. She held it in front of her, with both arms crossed over her chest as she turned to face him. "I'm sorry, Derek."

"Sorry for what?"

"For not following any of your security protocols last night. For bringing you out here so late." She glanced toward the window and saw the first rays of sun peeking over the horizon. "I mean, so early."

That was it; he couldn't keep away from her anymore. Reaching out, he caught her by the shoulder. "I don't give a rip about the security protocols. The most important thing is that you're all right."

A muscle in her temple fluttered, and he moved his hand to the nape of her neck. Gently, he rubbed his thumb against her racing pulse. "*Are* you okay, Shea?"

She swallowed hard and nodded.

He brushed the pad of his thumb along her jawline, and she straightened her spine. She nodded again and then moved by him. He got the door for her, and it seemed only right to settle his hand against the small of her back. When she didn't pull away, he left it there. Together, they walked out to the parking lot.

"He was over there," she said, pointing to the Dumpster. "Dressed all in black."

As they headed that way, the door to the adjacent office building opened. Phillip Morrison stepped outside, looking tall, handsome, and concerned. He quickly joined them. "Figure anything out?"

As much as he hated doing it, Derek pulled his hand away from Shea's back. "She's just walking me through what happened."

Shea stepped away to stand by Phillip, who swung his arm around her shoulders. Derek's hand automatically curled into a fist. He wanted to rip Phillip's arm right out of its socket. Where had Mr. Comfort been last night when she'd needed him? She'd had a nightmare, and the guy had let her walk away from their bed? He'd let her drive across town to be alone? What kind of a relationship was that?

Phillip cleared his throat. "Uh, do you think it was just a passerby, Derek?" He nodded toward the trash bin. "Strange place for a late-night walk."

"Is Biodermatics still shredding its documents like I recommended?"

"We try, but some things might slip through. Why?"

Shea looked at the trash bin, and her eyes widened. "You think he was going through our trash."

Derek glanced at her, pleased that they were on the same wavelength. He'd noticed the twin lids hanging over the back of the Dumpster the moment she'd pointed it out. "Garbage companies like to keep these bins closed. It keeps the smell in, and rain and animals out. I'd say your unexpected visitor was Dumpster diving. You might have caught him in the act."

Phillip didn't look convinced. "Skin care is a competitive business, but do you really think somebody would go that far?"

Derek let one eyebrow lift. "What was your profit last quarter?"

The man grimaced. "Enough to hire Audrey Lowe for our commercials."

"And how much would Shea's medical applications bring in?"

Shea reached up to rub her forehead, and her partner patted her arm soothingly. Derek's hands fisted against his hips, and he turned to look at the Dumpster . . . and noticed a smudge of silver on its front. His forehead furrowed, and he looked quickly at Shea's car. "Did you hit this?"

"He startled me," she mumbled.

Phillip looked at her sharply. "Tell him the truth."

Finally, Shea's head came up. "The truth is, I almost hit the man. He probably has more against me than I have against him."

Derek walked toward the couple slowly, his attention only on Shea. "Did you get a good look at him?"

She shook her head and wrapped her arms around her waist. "He had his hood pulled up. I never saw his face. I was too busy peeling away."

Derek's muscles tightened. "That was the best thing you could have done."

"Absolutely." Phillip ran a gentle touch over her hair. When he caught Derek's look, though, his arm dropped to his side.

A car pulled into the parking lot just then, surprising them all. The sunrise was just shooting purples and pinks across the sky.

"It's Tamika," Phillip said.

Shea glanced over her shoulder. "She's awfully early."

Derek looked at his watch. Yes, especially considering what time she'd gotten to bed last night. He watched as his charge got out of her car, a heavy bag swung over one shoulder and a large cup of coffee in her hand. When she saw them, her eyebrows rose above her dark sunglasses.

"What's going on?" she asked. Her voice sounded husky and unused.

".We had an intruder last night," Phillip said.

Tamika stopped mid step. Lifting her sunglasses to the top of her head, she gave them a worried look. Yet, it was a tired look, too. Her eyelids were heavy and her eyes lacked their normal luster. "Who was it? I mean . . . What did they want?"

"We don't know." Shea frowned. "Did you skip your run this morning?"

"Uh, yeah." Tamika shifted her bag on her shoulder. "I'm not training right now. Too busy."

Doing what? Derek wondered.

"Have you noticed anyone snooping around here lately?" he asked. "Have you taken any strange calls?"

"Strange calls? *Oh* yeah." Tamika gestured with her coffee, showing some of her normal spunk. "That pushy woman you want to hire is getting on my last nerve."

"What pushy woman?" Phillip asked.

"Lynette Fromm."

"I'm sure she's just excited at the prospect of getting back into her field," Shea said calmly.

"I didn't realize you needed a degree in chemistry to work in a business office." Tamika pulled her sunglasses back down, and her scowl darkened.

"We'll make a decision on that soon," Phillip promised. "But this matter has to take priority over everything else."

Like it hadn't already? Derek bit back a cutting remark when he saw the look on Shea's face. She was staring at the Dumpster and clutching her lab book protectively.

"I really don't care if somebody steals my work as long as it gets out there to help people." She swallowed hard. "I just need to know that my data won't be corrupted or lost. We've got to make sure that doesn't happen. Please, Derek."

When she asked him like that, he was ready to surround the place with armored tanks. "I'll take it on personally," he promised.

She looked at him swiftly. "Oh, I didn't mean that. I'm sure one of your staff would be just fine."

"You need *me*."

"But you have your company to run."

"I always do your work myself," he said, letting his voice drop. "You know that."

Phillip's eyebrows rose, and Tamika watched the scene with interest. Phillip caught her by the arm, and together they moved away.

Shea shifted uncomfortably. "I think this was just an isolated incident, Derek."

"I'll be very happy if you're right." He stepped closer. "I don't like it that someone was nosing around here, for any reason. I'm going to look into this whether you pay me to or not."

Her blue-eyed gaze locked with his.

"You need me," he told her bluntly. "And like it or not, you've got me."

"Wow," Phillip said as Derek's dark SUV pulled out of the parking lot. "I don't know if I just got singed or frostbitten."

Shea looked at her partner. "What are you talking about?"

"The looks he was giving me. What's going on between you two?"

"Between Derek and me? Nothing."

Tamika nearly choked on her coffee. "You call that 'nothing'? I want some of that 'nothing'!"

"Me, too." Phillip grinned. "Does he have any more brothers?"

Heat crawled up into Shea's neck. She'd thought she was the only one who'd noticed that Derek had been even more intense than usual. The waves of energy coming off him had been powerful—and sexy as sin.

When he'd helped her take off her lab jacket, she'd almost melted. All she'd been able to think about was her dream and the way he'd held her, kissed her, and fondled her breasts. . . .

"Hello? Earth to Shea," Tamika said.

"Is there anything you want to tell me?" Phillip asked. "What happened at that meeting yesterday?"

"I'm not sure," she said, dragging a hand through her hair. She'd always been aware of Derek, but now . . . She'd worried that letting him see her at less than full strength would damage his impression of her. Instead, it was as if her vulnerability brought out his protective side.

Phillip was still looking toward the road. "I don't envy that prowler, I'll tell you that. It wouldn't surprise me if he tracked down the guy's name, address, social security number, and shoe size. He has the skills to back up that macho attitude." He winked at Shea. "Lucky girl."

Her cheeks grew hotter. "The Industrial Park's security staff is looking into it, too."

Tamika looked at them, stunned. "How serious is this?"

Phillip's expression hardened. "Shea's lab might have been compromised."

Their assistant nodded slowly. "I'll go make more coffee."

Turning on her heel, she strode toward the office's door.

Phillip watched until she was inside, then turned to Shea. "He wants you."

Shea took a step back, startled. "I—"

"Wants you *bad*. I thought he might chew my arm off when I put it around your shoulders."

"So why didn't you let me go?"

Her partner smiled. "To see how far I could push him. Which wasn't much—he had me shaking in my shoes without even a word."

Derek could do that, Shea thought. With just a look, he could make her shiver, cause her nipples to pucker and her pussy to squeeze. Flustered, she smoothed a hand over her skirt.

"So that's the way it is, huh?" Phillip's grin got wider. "Well, as far as I'm concerned, it's about time."

She looked up quickly.

"You look at him the way you look at Baby Ruth candy bars—like you want him, but won't let yourself have him. And the way he looks at you, I'm surprised he hasn't taken you right down to the floor in front of everyone."

"Phillip!"

"You know I'm right, Shea. You two have been quietly wanting each other forever. I just don't understand why he's held back." Phillip tilted his head, watching her speculatively. "Something's changed."

Shea's grip tightened on her lab book. Her partner could back her into a corner when she least wanted it. "He's concerned about a possible breakdown in our security protocol."

"He's concerned about *you*."

"Semantics."

"I don't think so." Phillip crossed his arms over his chest, settling in like he always did when he got stubborn. "Why didn't you tell him the whole story?"

A warning tingle ran down her spine. "We told him everything he needs to know."

Nobody knew the whole truth—not even Phillip. Oh, he knew about her sleepwalking, but she'd never told him her deepest, darkest secret—her belief that her nighttime actions were not her own. Every time she thought about what could have happened last night, it nearly made her sick. Her Somnambulist could have made her burn down the entire building.

It had happened once before.

Her throat thickened. As a child, she remembered waking up and finding herself completing strange tasks like making banana and teabag sandwiches, or stacking

all her clothes in the middle of her bed. The disorienta-
tion had always been the worst, especially if she woke up
in strange rooms or closets. It was why she feared the
dark so badly.

Yet nothing had been as horrible as waking up with
night dew coating her skin, smoke filling her lungs,
and the sound of metal popping in her ears. Her family had lost its home that night. Their trailer had been
a total loss, but the price her dad had paid was even
steeper.

Tears blurred her vision as she looked at her building, at everything she'd worked so hard to achieve. Had
her Somnambulist been trying to do it again? Was that
why it was back?

She felt herself wobble.

Phillip caught her arm and led her toward the monu-
ment sign that boasted the Biodermatics name. Gently,
he made her sit down on the sign's base. "Ah, sweet-
heart. You've got to get some decent sleep."

She ground her teeth together. Did he think she
didn't know that? "I will," she said determinedly. "I've
got an appointment next week with my doctor."

Every problem had an answer. Sometimes you just
had to go after it with systematic, logical steps. She'd
been a child the last time her Somnambulist had come
calling. She was an adult now, and a highly trained scientist. She just needed to keep a cool head and think
objectively.

"I still think you should tell Derek," Phillip said dog-
gedly.

She gave him a hard look. "What would that accomplish?"

"If he knew, it might help him separate your actions from the prowler's. Your story didn't exactly add up. You didn't see the way he looked at you when you couldn't give him more details—not to mention the fact that hitting the Dumpster with your car isn't like you."

"Enough," she said, lifting her hand to stop him. "We're not telling him. He doesn't need to know."

"But he *wants* to know; it's clear on his face. Why don't you let him in, Shea? He's a good guy. You don't always have to be perfect."

"I'm not perfect. I'm not even close." And unfortunately, her particular flaw was more dangerous than most people's.

She let out a ragged breath. All the literature warned that sleepwalking adults could be even more volatile than sleepwalking children. There had been cases of people becoming violent with loved ones, having sex with strangers, or even committing murder while they were asleep. Her Somnambulist had already taken her driving. She hated to think about how bad it could get.

"Did you ever think your sleepwalking could be the result of something as simple as stress or sexual frustration?" Phillip tapped her on the knee. "Maybe it would calm you down to have Derek in your bed—or at the very least, tire you out."

Shea's skin prickled, the chill going straight to the bone despite the summer morning heat. As much as the idea turned her on, she couldn't even let her mind go there. Everyone was vulnerable while they were asleep—even a strong, competent man like Derek.

Look what she'd done to her father!

Her fingers curled into the cement. She'd come very close to hitting that trespasser last night. She couldn't bear to think of waking and finding Derek in her headlights.

Or worse.

"He can work on the prowler issue," she whispered. "Everything else is off-limits to him."

Until she found a way to regain control of her own body, she couldn't let him get near her. Nobody was safe—not while her Somnambulist was around.

Five

It was early Sunday morning when Derek arrived at IHOP for breakfast. As soon as he set foot inside the front door, the scent of pancakes and bacon wafted over him. He inhaled appreciatively, but surveyed the restaurant with a critical eye.

He and his brothers had their weekly get-togethers when the crowds were low; they needed the privacy to talk about Dream Wreaker business. Right now, two tables of night shift workers were grabbing a bite to eat before they went home to bed. Up front, a trucker was getting ready to hit the road. Other than that, business was slow. The after-church crowd wouldn't arrive for a while.

Apparently, neither would his family.

Glancing at his watch, Derek realized he was early. Irritated, he tugged at his shirt cuffs. He still hadn't been able to make contact with Zane, and he wanted to talk with his delinquent brother one-on-one. Too bad he usually strolled in after the rest of them had placed their orders.

"Morning, Derek," Sally called as she came through the swinging door that led to the kitchen. The pretty blonde was one of their regular waitresses. "Want some coffee?"

"Bring a pot."

"Oooh," she said with a wink. "Long night?"

"Long week."

"I pushed two tables together for you guys. Will that be enough?"

"If it's not, we can help ourselves."

"Thanks, hon." She smiled and walked past him with a steaming order of eggs and hash browns hoisted up near her shoulder. "I'll bring that coffee to you in a minute."

Derek nodded, impatience eating at him. He really didn't have time for this today. He was busy looking for evidence that one of Biodermatics's competitors might have gotten their hands on Shea's proprietary data. He'd talked with the garbage company and determined when they'd made their last pickup. He'd also spoken with the Bio staff to learn what might have been in jeopardy during that time frame. And he'd already been on the computer this morning, checking again to make sure none of the company's data had been tampered with.

For probably the first time ever, he didn't want to be here, ancient duty or not.

Unfortunately, Shea wasn't his only concern.

Pulling out a chair, he sat and straightened his tie, readying himself for business. Things hadn't yet settled down in the nighttime world. The people of Solstice were still having problems sleeping, including Tamika Hendricks, who was calling for him later and later every night. Was it a coincidence Shea's secretary was also having sleep problems, or was he missing something entirely?

He and his brothers needed to keep each other updated on what was happening so they wouldn't be caught off-guard. Again.

"Here you go," Sally said as she brought the promised coffee. "And look what I found."

On her heels were two of his younger brothers—neither of which was Zane.

"Hey, Derek," Wes said as he sat down across the table. "How's it going?"

AJ just nodded.

"Busy," Derek said succinctly. "Do you guys know if Zane is coming?"

"There's food, so it's probably a good bet." Wes leaned back in his chair so Sally could pour him some joe. "Why? You need to talk to him?"

"Yeah."

His brother's eyebrows rose. "What did he do this time?"

"Nothing, maybe. I'm not sure." Derek took a slow drink from his own cup, trying to remain objective. He didn't know if Zane was to blame for Shea's problem or not. He didn't even know what her problem was—and that was driving him crazy. He was the guy everyone always turned to for help. He was the one who always got answers. Unfortunately, she was only turning to him about work issues.

She had Phil for everything else.

"Whew," Wes said. "Whatever Zane did, it must be bad."

Derek rubbed his hand over the back of his neck. "I just need to talk to him, the sooner the better."

He looked to AJ, trying to concentrate on someone who *was* his charge. "Do you know Tamika Hendricks? Tall, beautiful black woman who runs in those 5K races you do?"

AJ's head snapped up. "Long legs?"

"That's the one."

His brother fingered his fork carefully. "I might know who you're talking about. She didn't run yesterday, though. I haven't seen her for a while."

That was what Derek had been worried about. When Tamika was training, she slept like a baby. For her not to be running at all . . . Something was up.

"Everything okay with her?" AJ asked.

"Maybe. She's not getting a lot of sleep. Can you keep an eye out for her? See if she shows up on the running paths?"

AJ nodded, muttering "I always do."

"Hey!" Wes suddenly scooted his chair back and stood. "Look who's here!"

Derek looked quickly to his left, hoping it was Zane making an unexpected early appearance. It wasn't.

Tony had brought Cael.

"Hey," Derek said, pleasantly surprised. "You made it."

"I'm not an invalid, Wes," Cael complained as their younger brother pulled out the chair at the head of the table for him. Still, he sank into the seat a bit gingerly. "Thanks."

"How are you doing?" Derek asked.

"Better. A lot better." Cael looked more comfortable now that he'd taken a seat. Derek knew that he'd been pushing the physical therapy to the limits, but it would take a while before he was back to one hundred percent.

"Big brother was out on the curb waiting for me," Tony said, taking the seat on the opposite side of the table. "I think he has ants in his pants."

"Let's hope he's got a little more than *that* for Sexy Red."

Cael stiffened as the dry comment came over his head. Zane had arrived, attitude intact. He cuffed their oldest brother on the shoulder affectionately before taking the chair on Derek's right.

"Is there a problem with your cell phone?" Derek asked as Zane leaned forward for the pot of coffee. "I've been trying to get in touch with you."

His brother looked at him and let out a snort. His eyes danced with unexplained humor, but then he muttered something that sounded like, "Nah, too easy."

"I lost the thing," he said with a shrug. "Somewhere on that pub crawl Wednesday night, I think."

Sally showed up with her order pad at the ready. She placed a hand on Cael's shoulder and squeezed. "It's good to see you, hon. The girls here all missed you."

"Aren't we enough for you, Sal?" Tony put a pout on his face. Somehow, it didn't match the massive biceps stretching the sleeves of his T-shirt.

"Oh, you're all dreamboats, and you know it," she teased.

"Dreamboats," Wes said with a smile on his face. He let out a laugh, and AJ quickly elbowed him.

"Are you guys ready to order?"

Derek sighed. So much for his one-on-one time with Zane. Now he'd have to wait until after breakfast. Reining in his exasperation, he folded his menu.

One by one, they went around the table, ending with Tony who got teased when he placed a side order for "girly" peach crepes.

Derek just couldn't laugh with the rest of his brothers. His brain was churning over other things, like Shea hitting that Dumpster. It didn't make sense. Had she tried to run the guy down? That didn't sound like her at all, unless it had something to do with the fear he'd seen in her eyes at his office. Was someone threatening her?

The thought was like a hot poker in his gut. He needed some answers *now*.

"Can we get this meeting called to order?" he asked the moment Sally was out of earshot.

Zane looked his way. "Looks like Cael's not the only one with ants in his pants."

"Zip it, Zane." Derek had waited as long as he could. "How are things going on your rounds?"

His brother's forehead furrowed. "Fine. What's up with you?"

"Are you sure there isn't anything unusual going on?"

"Unusual?" Understanding lit his brother's eyes, and he smiled. "You don't want to have this conversation with me here."

Derek scowled. The hell he didn't. If something was going on during his rounds as a Dream Wreaker, they all should know. "Are you having problems?"

"No." Zane's congenial mood started to harden. "But it sure sounds like you are."

Their stares locked, neither of them willing to back down.

"Just ease up on the nightmares, okay?" Derek said softly. "I'm talking about Shea Caldwell."

Zane set down his cup with a clatter, splashing coffee onto the table. "I know exactly who you're talking about. And while they may be nightmares to me, she seems to get off on them."

That was it. Derek turned so that they were nose to nose. "Just stop playing with her head. It might be fun for you to toy with some of your other charges, but you will not do this to her. You hear me?"

"Hey," Tony snapped from across the table. "Keep it down. And who's 'her'?"

Neither Derek nor Zane paid him any attention. Their stares were locked and unblinking.

"What are you accusing me of, Mr. By-the-Book?" Zane asked.

"She's feeling the effects," Derek growled. "You need to back off."

Zane knocked his fist against the table, making even the carousel of syrups jump. "I don't know what you're talking about. She's had one nightmare—and it didn't start out that way. I haven't been leading her."

"Then what the hell is going on?"

His brother laughed, the sound sharp and humorless. "If you don't know, I'm certainly not going to tell you."

"Whoa." Cael's fingers bit into Derek's shoulder when he started to lunge forward; his grip tough and his voice stern. "What's going on here?"

Looking around, Derek saw that everyone had stopped talking and was staring at them—including the trucker at the front table.

"A client of mine has been having trouble sleeping," he said tightly. "She won't tell me exactly what the problem is, but she's tense and scared." He looked pointedly to his right. "And she's Zane's charge."

"So it's my fault?"

Derek let silence answer for him.

Zane's face turned belligerent. "If it's anyone's fault, it's yours."

He sat forward and poked Derek in the chest. "She's dreaming, all right, but those so-called nightmares are about you, buddy boy. She's having erotic dreams about the two of you together. Hot, get naked, heavy petting, erotic dreams."

Derek caught the finger and was ready to cause some major pain when the words sank into his brain.

And froze it.

His little brother gave him another nudge. "God, I've never known you to be dense before. Do you need me to spell it out? She wants you, Derek. That's probably why she's getting all tense and weird around you."

Tony leaned forward with a grin. "What's her name again?"

Zane yanked his finger out of Derek's limp grip and folded his arms triumphantly across his chest. "Shea Caldwell."

"Shea. Anyone got anything?" Tony looked around for input.

Whispers went back and forth. Still, Derek couldn't move. *Shea was dreaming about him?*

"Co-owner and head research scientist for Biodermatics, Inc.," Zane supplied.

"Biodermatics," Wes repeated. "That's the company with the commercial with all those sexy women. The one where they lie back, point their toes in the air, and smooth that stuff all over their legs. Hey, is she in it?"

"No!" Derek snapped, finally coming out of his stupor.

"No way. She's top grade all the way," Zane agreed. "Classy, quiet, and smart as a whip. But if she'd wanted to be in that commercial, she would have rocked it."

Tony's eyebrows rose. "So she's a looker?"

"Blonde and flat-out gorgeous."

Cael leaned forward onto his elbows. He looked as pleased as the rest of them, but the expression was tempered with concern. "Derek, what's wrong with you? You usually read people like books."

Derek felt like he was swirling; his thoughts, his head, his body . . . Then that one, all-too-important fact slammed into his head, shutting everything down, leaving him cold. "She's taken," he said flatly.

None of this mattered. Hell yeah, it gave him a boner to know she was dreaming about him. But thinking about that would just give him a hard cock *and* a headache.

"No, she's not," Zane said, taken aback.

Derek looked at him so quickly, he nearly wrenched his neck. "Yes, she is. Her partner. Phillip."

Zane shook his head. "She sleeps alone—in some mighty sexy lingerie, I might add."

Derek had his hand fisted in his brother's T-shirt before he knew it. "Phillip Morrison. They've been together since college."

"Morrison?" AJ shook his head. "No. He's one of mine. They're not together."

"But—"

"He's gay."

"What?" Derek's fist dropped from Zane's shirt.

"Mostly closeted, but gay." AJ shrugged.

For the second time in one minute, Derek couldn't think. There wasn't one clear thought in his head.

Cael's voice cut through the haze. "What are you still doing here?"

Derek looked at him blankly.

"Do you want her, or not?"

Everything clicked into place, and Derek's chair skidded back. "I've got to go."

Laughter, hoots, and words of encouragement erupted from the table, drawing the attention of the growing crowd. Sally skidded to a halt with their order lifted high on her shoulder as Derek strode past. He slapped a ten spot on the counter by the cash register and reached into his pocket for his keys as he headed out the door.

He didn't see his brothers smiling behind him.

Tony tapped Cael on the shoulder as they watched Derek's car peel out of the parking lot. "I told you so."

"It's about time that guy got laid," Zane said dryly. "He's wound tighter than a spring."

Cael turned on their little brother. He might have been out of action for a while, but he wasn't weak. "Were you telling the truth? Did you do anything to influence those dreams?"

"Like I'd have her dream about him instead of me." Zane ran a hand over his ruffled hair, obviously more affected by the confrontation than he wanted to admit. "Close it down. Here's our food."

Tony got up to help Sally, who was still looking curiously at the front door.

"Is something wrong?" she asked.

"Nah," he answered. "Something's very right."

They served breakfast and Sally finally moved away, picking up the money Derek had left at the register.

The moment she was gone, Wes sat forward. "You can't leave us hanging. Tell us more."

Zane took a bite of bacon and shook his head in disbelief. "When that little gem of a movie first started playing in her head, it about knocked me out of my boxers. At first I thought Derek had something to do with it. You know, like he was pulling some kind of long distance trick you guys haven't told me about?" He rolled his eyes. "But then I remembered I was thinking about The Machine."

Tony ran his thumb against his lower lip. "Do you think there's something else going on with her, though? He seemed to think she was having sleep problems."

Zane's brown eyes lost their twinkle, and the perpetual smile on his face faded. "Maybe. She's gotten very unpredictable. I find her sleeping in odd places, or she doesn't call for REM sleep until late in the night. Something's going on; I just don't know what it is. I was going to ask you guys about it today. Tactfully, though."

"That's you, all right. Mr. Tactful." Tony glanced toward the door and shifted his shoulders uncomfortably. "I've never seen Derek like that before. Is she really worth all the drama?"

"Oh, *yeah*," Zane said without hesitation. "Totally drama worthy."

Six

The morning sun was bright as Shea came down the stairs but to her, it might as well have been the pitch of night.

It had gotten to her again.

Her hand clenched the banister tightly, bracing herself as she took one step down and then another. Every muscle in her body was tense. Half of her wanted to hurry, to just get it over with, but the other half held back, afraid of what she might find downstairs.

She'd woken up in her closet, clutching her fire extinguisher to her chest.

As if that weren't enough to send her into a blind panic, a trail of her shoes led out the door. She was following them now—out of her bedroom, down the hall, and down the stairs. The placement was methodical. Left, right, left, right . . . All in pairs. It was almost as if she were following the Invisible Woman's footsteps. Where did they lead? And why?

Holding the extinguisher under her arm, she sniffed the air and listened intently. Her feet touched the plush carpet at the bottom landing, and her toes dug in. Taking a ragged breath, she did a quick check of her living room. The coffee table in front of her sofa was cluttered with industry magazines and reference books. Her laptop was lying askew in front of the chair, open but powered down. The television remote was propped up on the windowsill.

Everything was in its place, as she'd left it . . . except for the trail of shoes that led into the kitchen.

She moved deeper into the room, the pathway calling to her. "Please not the basement," she whispered. "*Not* the basement."

She turned into the kitchen and stopped.

The trail ended in front of the kitchen sink with her favorite pair of shoes, blue-and-white zebra-striped stilettos. They were lined up next to each other facing the sink. It was as if she'd stood staring out the window—and washing it down with the sprayer from the faucet?

Dear Lord, there was water everywhere.

Snapping out of it, she put the fire extinguisher on the counter and grabbed the dishrag. She wiped up the puddles as best as she could.

Why had it done this? Was there a message here? What could it possibly be trying to tell her? It made no sense.

But when did it ever?

Her chest tightened. After the sleep driving incident, she'd started taking something to help her sleep. She'd hoped the pills would ward off her unwanted night visitor, but they'd only given her a two-night reprieve.

She'd known better than to let them make her com-
placent.

She rubbed her bare arms, fear clouding her brain.
Anger worked just as hard to clear it. How many trips
had it taken to bring all those shoes down? And the
snow boots on the stairs had to have come from storage
downstairs.

How long had it had control of her?

"God help me," she whispered, bracing her hands
against the counter. She needed to move up that appointment with Dr. Wainright. The scientist inside her told
her she had a sleep disorder, a bad one.

She just couldn't quiet the words in the back of her
mind, the curse that had been hissed at her so long
ago.

Demon child. Demon child!

Mrs. Lupescu had insisted she was possessed.

Shea shook her head. She didn't want to go there.
She didn't want to remember. Yet the more she tried to
push the memory away, the clearer it got.

*Shea didn't know what awakened her, the noises or the hard-
ness of her bed. Her eyes felt heavy as she tried to open them,
but the noises wouldn't let her go back to sleep. Loud cracks
and pops sounded in her ears, but it was the howling of her
alarm clock that made her groan. It was too early to get up
for school. She felt like she'd just fallen asleep.*

*Groaning, she stretched. The sheets of her bed scratched
and clung to her hair. She pushed them away, but her hand
came away wet and dirty.*

Her eyes popped open. Darkness pressed down on her, the air sticky and heavy. It caught in her throat as she bolted upright. Her heart pounded as she looked around, disoriented. She'd done it again. She'd walked in her sleep, and this time she'd wandered outside!

Standing up, she frantically brushed the dirt off of herself, trying to get a fix on where she was. It felt like she was in a hole, but she could see bright lights up higher. Lights flashed in reds and blues, and suddenly she recognized the wailing of her alarm clock for what it was. A siren!

Something was wrong, very wrong.

Stumbling, she headed for the bright, flickering light that seemed to be in the center of it all. The ground was uneven, though, and her feet slipped on the dirt and grass. She finally realized why she was so much lower than everything else; she was in the ditch! Turning, she scrambled up the slope.

The moment she came topside, she knew where she was. Guiltily, she looked down. She was right in the middle of Mrs. Lupescu's prized herb garden. She scrambled to the side, but not before a puff of wind betrayed her, ringing the bells that hung over the woman's door.

Out in front of the trailer, she saw a flurry of movement. Shea cringed, recognizing the flare of her neighbor's full skirt. She tried to avoid the rosemary, but Mrs. Lupescu gasped when she saw her. The woman's face paled, and Shea's chin wobbled.

"I'm sorry," she said, tiptoeing out of the garden. "I didn't mean to."

"Dear Lord," Mrs. Lupescu breathed. Her dark ringlets swung as she looked toward the bright, flickering light and

then back to Shea. Muttering under her breath, she reached into her pocket and clumsily pulled out a piece of bread. She held it out in warning. "Stay away from me."

Shea didn't understand. Mrs. Lupescu carried bread to ward off evil spirits, but she wasn't evil. "Mrs. Lupescu? What's wrong?"

"You demon child! That Somnambulist has gotten hold of you. Stay back."

Shea froze, the awful words going right to her stomach. Her neighbor had told her stories of Somnambulists and night spirits, but she'd never looked at her like this before. "What happened?" she asked, her voice tiny.

"Demon," the widow hissed. She waved the bread in warning. "Demon child!"

Shea took a step forward and the woman backed up. Another step, and the woman turned and ran. Shea's legs felt like noodles as she walked toward the front of the trailer and the main road. The hair on the back of her neck rose. It was bad. Whatever had happened, she knew it was bad.

The crowd blocked her view, but above their heads she saw the fire. Flames shot into the air, bright against the black sky, all oranges and reds and yellows. The way they danced took her breath away.

Demon child.

The accusation rang in her ears. Oh, no. Please don't let her have done this. Please!

Her leaden legs carried her forward, and she weaved in and out of gawkers watching the scene. She had an awful feeling in her gut, a terrible cold sensation. She squeezed between a policeman and a fire truck and her mouth dropped open.

Her trailer. It was her home!

"Shea!"

It took a second to recognize her dad's voice; he sounded frantic. She opened her mouth to respond, but smoke blew into her face, choking her throat and grabbing her lungs.

"Shea? Are you still in there?"

She pushed her way through the crowd and saw her dad kicking at their trailer's door. A fireman tried to pull him away, but he kept screaming her name.

"Dad!" she choked out.

With the sirens and the fire, he didn't hear her.

"Dad, I'm here!" She started to run toward him, but she screamed when the door gave way and her dad rushed into the shuddering, flaming mass of metal. "No! No!"

"No," Shea repeated, pulling back from the nightmare. "No!"

A cold, helpless feeling came over her, cinching her ribs until she could hardly breathe. It was a feeling she remembered all too well, a feeling she'd always hated. She rubbed her breastbone, trying to ease the ache, and forcibly kicked the memory out of her head. She wasn't a child anymore. She could deal with this.

She *had* to deal with this.

Focusing determinedly, she bent down and picked up her zebra stilettos. Her hands were clumsy, and she nearly dropped them. Standing straight, she forced herself to take deep, calming breaths.

She had a problem, and problems could be solved by taking logical, sequential steps. So she'd move up her appointment with Dr. Wainright and schedule a visit to the Solstice Sleep Clinic.

She *would* take care of this.

Following the trail in reverse direction, she swept up as many shoes into her arms as she could. She'd barely climbed halfway up the staircase, though, when a pounding at her front door made her jump. The sound was loud and demanding, much too insistent for so early on a weekend morning.

The jackhammer sound lifted a warning flag in her head. Oh, God—had she done something far worse than an impromptu footwear show?

Dropping the shoes over the railing, she hurried down to the front door. Her heart was in her throat as she looked through the eyepiece.

She nearly came right out of her nightie when she saw Derek bearing down on her.

And he looked *riled*.

Her mouth went dry. She could see the fierceness in the line of his jaw. His eyes sparked of midnight, his dark hair was rumpled, and his impatience radiated right through the door.

Her hand went to her chest. *What had happened? What had he found?*

"Shea! Open this door!"

"Oh, God." Please don't let anything have happened to her research. Or her buildings. Or her friends . . .

Sliding the chain lock off its mooring, she opened the door against her chest. "Derek, what's wrong? Why are you here?"

His dark gaze fixed on her, and her heart did that funny stutter inside her chest again. He had a hand propped against each side of the doorjamb and his body was so tense, his muscles looked ready to explode. "Why did you let me think you and Phillip were together?" he asked.

Shea blinked at the odd question, trying to pull her scattered thoughts together. "We *are* together. We're partners."

"Business partners," he said, his voice like a knife.

She didn't understand what he was getting at, but his anger and impatience had the morning air crackling. Something had rocked him off his calm—and she could feel him all the way to her core. Her belly squeezed, and she pressed herself tightly against the shield of the door. "Yes," she said, her voice going unnaturally quiet. "What does that have to do with anything?"

"Not bed partners," he said, ignoring her question.

She nearly lost her grip on the doorknob. "Of course not. I never— Why would you—"

She didn't know how he moved so fast. One moment, he was outside her door. The next, he was inside her home.

Shea gasped and pulled the door open wide, squeezing herself between it and the wall. In just her nightie, she felt vulnerable and exposed.

On edge, she stared at him. His hair looked as if he'd raked his hands through it a couple dozen times, and his suit jacket was almost as rumpled. It sat crooked on his wide shoulders, straining under the tension in those thick muscles. Most telling, though, his tie was almost undone and his collar was loosened.

She'd always wondered what would happen if he stepped outside his business persona. She had the sinking, thrilling feeling that she was about to find out.

"Why the big façade?" he demanded.

"*What* façade? I don't know what you're talking about."

"Were you trying to keep me at arm's length?"

"No!" *Maybe.*

He took a step forward. "Because if that was your goal, you're going to have to stop looking at me like that."

Sexual excitement oozed through Shea's body, and her nipples hardened almost unbearably.

Derek swore and raked a hand through his hair, mussing it even more. Making her want to give it a try . . .

"I said stop—" He went dead still when he caught a glimpse of what she was wearing. Muscle by muscle, his face crumpled. "Oh, *hell.*"

He moved like a blur again, and suddenly she felt the door's weight lessening against her . . . the handle slipping out of her damp palm . . . his hand catching her lower back . . . the nape of her neck . . .

And, oh God. His mouth came down hot against hers. His lips devoured her as his tongue pressed deep.

A moan rose from deep inside her throat, and all that fearful energy inside her changed to arousal, sharp and intense. He was offering her an escape, and she grabbed onto him with both hands. "Derek," she whispered.

The hand at the small of her back tightened, bringing her up solidly against him—and against a very thick, very hard erection.

He groaned as he turned them and leaned his shoulders back against the wall. The way he pulled her toward him had her rocking up on her tiptoes, off balance. He took her weight easily as he kissed her again, harder, with more hunger.

"So good," he murmured against her lips. "Why did you try to put the brakes on this? Why?"

"I didn't—" She gasped when his hands ran from her waist to her thighs. The sensation of his touch against her bare flesh was startling. "You just always . . . put me off-kilter. . . . It's . . . *ahhh* . . . intimidating."

His head snapped back, and his hands froze against her.

"Not in a bad way," she rushed to say. "You just always watch me so closely."

His dark eyes narrowed.

"Like that," she whispered, shifting uncomfortably.

The move rubbed her stomach more intimately against him, and instinctively, his hips swiveled with hers.

"Can't be helped," he said raspily.

She bit her lip when his hands started moving again. They brushed against the back of her thighs, making her skin tingle as if it were electrified. When his teeth caught her earlobe in a sharp pinch, she shuddered.

"You look at me the same way," he said, soothing the hurt with a sweep of his tongue. "The only difference is that you try to hide it."

She shivered as his hands swept upward again, this time under her nightie. His blunt fingers traced the crease where her legs met the curve of her bottom, and she let out a soft cry as she unexpectedly creamed. The hot *whoosh* of excitement poured out of her, making her realize just how serious things were getting.

And how out of control she was, too.

She caught his wrists as his thumbs hooked around the thin elastic bands at her hips. "I don't know—"

"Yes, you do."

He stole another quick kiss. When his hands began their determined sweep downward, her panties went with them. Their gazes connected as the little scrap of nothing slid over her knees and down to the floor.

"It's time," he said firmly.

He caught her chemise and tugged it upward. The ice-blue silk went sailing, and Shea suddenly found herself standing naked with her arms raised sexily over her head.

Derek's gaze swept down her body, his concentration never more intense, and a tight, urgent ball of need gelled in her stomach. Her nipples beaded tightly under that determined look and, for a second, she thought she felt his hands tremble against her waist. Then they were sliding over the curves of her bottom to determinedly grip the backs of her thighs.

She let out a short cry of surprise when he picked her up. He just spread her legs and lifted her. She grasped at his shoulders and wrapped her legs around his waist to keep her balance.

"No more holding me off," he said, dropping kisses onto her shoulder. Down below, he rubbed her butt possessively, his fingers dipping deeper into the crack of her ass with every pass.

"No more of the 'strictly business' routine," he ordered as he carried her into the living room. "And if you need help, you call *me*."

Shea started tugging at his clothes. She wanted him naked. Before she could get more than his tie off, though, he laid her down and stepped back.

Her breaths seized inside her chest when she looked up at him.

He was standing over her in the bright morning sunlight, looking like something she only saw in her nighttime dreams. His face was hard. His muscled chest expanded and contracted with each ragged breath. What caught her attention most, though, was the big, erect cock trying to find a way out of his pants.

"Derek," Shea said shakily.

His look was blistering hot as he began stripping out of his jacket and shirt. Her nipples tightened so hard they hurt. This was all so fast. So unexpected. So out of character for him.

Or maybe she was just seeing the real him, the side that wasn't kept lashed down and tied up in rules.

The side that was straining to get out.

God, she knew what that felt like.

He went for the zipper of his pants. "You've had me worried as hell."

He was naked before she could process the words—

and then, looking at him, she couldn't think at all. He was built, *GQ underwear model built.*

"I need you to talk to me," he whispered as he grasped her ankles in each hand.

Shea's heart began to pound, a hard, desperate thudding that made everything more vivid, more real.

This was just about as real as she could stand.

He determinedly spread her legs. Leaning down, he kissed her inner ankle.

"Oh, God," she said, her voice going tight.

His lips slid ever so slowly up her shin, and his tongue swirled around her kneecap. "I need you to trust me."

"I do trust you."

"Not enough," he said. His mouth moved up her leg, sliding with purpose to her quaking inner thigh muscles.

"Let me closer," he whispered. "I want to be closer."

She clutched for him. One hand found the top of his head. The other bit into the straining muscles of his shoulder. He nudged her legs wider to make room for himself.

"Trust me, Shea."

His hot breaths touched the most private part of her. Her back arched, but he pressed her back down. Catching her behind her knees, he lifted her legs up against her chest. Opening her. Displaying her.

"Let me in."

The first touch of his tongue blew her mind into a million pieces, sweeping across a place that was hidden and taboo. Her anus tightened under the wet, rough caress, but then it was gone, sliding slowly upward.

"I don't . . . I can't . . ."

Her breaths heaved in her chest, fighting the weight of her legs, her excitement and her need. His devious tongue swept upward with a slowness that was driving her insane. Shea held on by a thread as he licked her pussy lips, probed her opening, and prodded her sensitive clit.

But then it was onward and upward.

"Ohhh," she groaned, so aroused she was shaking the entire couch.

Or maybe that was both of them.

Derek was trying so hard to keep himself contained, his muscles were jumping.

He'd never felt anything as intoxicating as Shea's skin. He couldn't get enough of it. Dipping his tongue into her belly button, he gave it a swirl. She shivered against his face, making him just want to rear up and plunge into her.

But there was so much more to explore, so much more to revel in. He wet his tongue and gave her belly one long, destroying lick.

He wanted her so badly he was nearly going blind. She was so stunningly perfect. He let his weight come down on her more heavily, and he hissed as she touched him everywhere. His shoulders, his back, his ass . . .

He hovered over her breasts, trying to slow down, but it just wasn't going to happen.

"You're so beautiful," he said.

He finally gave in and did what he'd wanted to do forever. He licked. He stroked. He sucked. Her shoulders pressed so hard into the cushion, she met the boundaries of the spring-loaded base beneath it. Still, she stayed poised as his mouth came over her nipple and gave one hard pull.

"Ahh!" she cried.

He turned to the other one and suckled even harder, but he couldn't take much more foreplay. He felt like a racehorse heading down the straightaway.

And she was right there with him.

"Oh, please," she moaned, her body heaving beneath his.

Derek ran his hands up her sides as his mouth slid up her middle. Then he was finally over her, atop her completely. He settled into the cradle of her hips, his stomach pressing intimately against hers and his chest finding the cushion of her breasts.

He caught her hands and locked his fingers with hers, palm to palm. Their knuckles dug into the cushion on either side of her head, and he looked down at her. The head of his cock nudged at her opening, and she gave a soft whimper.

He just had to know one thing.

"Do you dream about me?"

"Yessss!"

He thrust into her everywhere at once: his tongue into her mouth, his cock into her pussy. The feel of her had him gasping for air. She was tight and white-hot. Her silky grip almost pushed him right over the edge, but then he felt her moan against his lips.

"Shea," he rasped.

The sturdy couch groaned under their moving bodies. Friction built between them, skittering along his skin. She was holding on to him with everything she had. Her fingers bit into the backs of his hands. Her legs wrapped around him high, catching him about the ribs. And her pussy—she gripped him hardest there.

"Oh, hell, baby."

Their bodies had wanted each other for too long; neither of them could take a drawn out seduction. It was a hot, fast, wet fuck that had them both panting and straining.

Shea's orgasm hit first. Her body arched, and she let out a cry as she tumbled into the abyss. Derek kept moving atop her, his cock going deeper and harder with every thrust.

"So good," he groaned, pressing his face into the crook of her neck. He couldn't get enough of her. He wanted this to go on forever. "Shea, I—"

Forever ended with a bang. He tensed, let out a yell, and exploded into her.

And that moment did seem like forever.

When he finally sank back onto her soft body, Derek's mind was blank. His tension and agitation were gone. That never-ending ache of wanting was eased. Nothing was pushing at him or demanding something from him. He relished emptiness for a long time, before he realized he didn't feel empty at all.

Gradually he eased his hold on Shea's hands, but he didn't let go. He rubbed his palms against hers, enjoying the sensation. Slowly, he lifted his head. She looked as stunned as he felt.

Stunned and more than a little self-conscious.

The room was suddenly very quiet. Sunlight streamed through the window as they studied each other, both achingly aware of what they'd done. What they were technically still doing . . .

Derek felt the muscles at the base of his spine tighten. This hadn't been his plan. It hadn't even been close. They'd ventured onto totally new ground here. Barreled onto it, actually, without thought or caution . . .

"You make me lose control," he said, surprised.

"Me, too," she whispered.

He never turned himself loose. It was just too . . . *hard.* Expectations always held him back. Responsibility. Yet, the moment he'd touched her, he hadn't been able to rein himself in. Even now, he was feeling the urge to start all over again. One signal, one touch, one look from her was all it would take.

But she seemed wary.

Squeezing her hands, he levered his chest off of her. The distance wasn't far enough so that their bodies weren't still intimately connected, but it was enough so she could breathe more easily. "I didn't mean to jump you like that," he said.

Her lips slowly parted. "Oh . . . that's . . . it's . . ."

"Like *that.* I came over here fully intending to bed you—I just should have said hello first."

"Oh," she said breathlessly.

The look on her face turned Derek's muscles to

putty. He couldn't help it. She was the most beautiful thing he'd ever seen, especially now with her body warm and welcoming under his . . . the sunlight glowing in her hair . . .

"Tell me you want this, too."

"I do," she said, pink coloring her cheeks. "I've been attracted to you since we first met."

"But?"

"But . . . it's not a good time for me to get involved with someone."

"Why not?" he asked pointedly.

"There's just . . . too much going on. The prowler, my research . . ."

Her gaze flicked across the room toward the staircase. Her pupils dilated and she quickly looked away, but not before he recognized the look. He'd seen that fear on her face before. He quickly followed her gaze, but all he saw was a pile of shoes on the floor.

"What's wrong, Shea?" His hands tightened on hers, and his body shifted instinctively, trying to cover her and protect her from harm. "Is someone threatening you? Why are you so scared?"

"Threatening me?" Her eyes widened. "No, it's nothing like that."

"Is it me?" he asked roughly, hating the idea. She had to know he'd never hurt her. He'd cut out his own heart before he'd do that. "I know I can be intense, but when I saw you dressed like that . . . and realized you weren't with Phillip . . ."

"Oh Derek, it's not you!"

He could see the turmoil on her face, but then her worried gaze dropped to his lips.

"It's *not* you."

She lifted her head and kissed him. The touch of her lips was gentle and erotic, and it melted him from the inside out. Entranced, he let go of her hands to slowly run his fingers up her arms and over her shoulders. She turned her head, adjusting the slant of her mouth across his, and his fingers fisted into her hair when he felt the soft lash of her tongue.

"*You* don't scare me, Derek. You just surprised me."

But something did scare her. This close, he could hear the emphasis she hadn't intended. He could see the slight widening of her eyes and feel the tension running underneath her skin. Her hands brushed against his back, and he made a decision fast.

"Spend the day with me."

It was impulsive and he hadn't thought everything through, but he didn't care. Hadn't he just learned that good things could happen when he didn't overanalyze them? That going with his instincts sometimes felt better than anything else in the world?

Shea glanced again toward the pile of shoes, but he caught her chin and made her look at him.

"You need to stop overthinking this, Madame Curie."

They both did.

Leaning down, he gave her a slow, hungry kiss. Rolling his hips, he lodged his growing erection inside her more deeply. "Ask me to stay—just for the day."

Her breath caught and her leg shifted sexily around his hip.

Derek's muscles tensed as he waited for her response. He'd just put himself out further on that limb—and her answer was a bit too slow in coming. He watched her closely, and the worry in her eyes cut too deep. Slowly, he started to pull away.

Her fingers dug into his back. "Stay."

He'd never gotten so hard so fast. "Where's the bed?"

Seven

He'd let her fall asleep.

It was the first clear thought that ran through Shea's mind when she opened her eyes. That, and the fact that Derek was still with her. His heat pressed against her back, and his arm draped heavily across her waist.

Even as she responded in pleasure, she tensed.

They'd spent the day making love, and now the sun was setting. Night was creeping in. Even the littlest thing could set her Somnambulist off, and today had been anything but normal. Yet she'd let herself be lulled into sleep. What had she been thinking?

"There you are," a deep voice rumbled. The hand against her stomach flexed, and she was pulled more tightly against the big male form behind her.

A muscled thigh slipped between her legs, and Shea arched as a soft kiss was placed at the side of her neck. Obviously she *hadn't* been thinking; her brain had been shorted out.

How could she have let her guard down like that?

The freedom had been fantastic, arousing and intoxicating. But how could she have forgotten what had been happening to her? What had happened just this morning?

Oh, God. Had she done anything in her sleep? With Derek here?

"How long have I been asleep?" she asked in a rush.

"Not long."

That rumbling voice was too sexy; she had to look into his eyes. Tucking the sheet up high under her arms, she rolled over to face him. When she did, her breath caught. His short hair was mussed and dark shadows lined his jaw. The bad boy look didn't fit his character, but it was so incredibly hot, she had to press her legs together.

Unable to help herself, she let her gaze drop. She took in the well-drawn lines of his body, his muscled chest and rippling abs, but the sheet sitting low on his hips wasn't what made her look up again. It was the relaxed look on his face. She'd never seen him so at ease in the moment. It made her belly warm.

Relaxed was good, right? If she'd gotten up and danced zombie pirouettes around the room, he wouldn't be relaxed.

Or so obviously ready to make love to her again.

"You were out like a light." His gaze slid over her face, alert as always. One of his eyebrows twitched when he saw the tension she was trying to hide. Reaching out, he caught her by the waist and pulled her back to him. "Maybe that last time in the shower was a bit too much."

Shea's racing thoughts skidded to a stop.

The shower.

She remembered that. She glanced over Derek's shoulder toward the bathroom, her body melting as memories flashed through her mind. She remembered how cool the tile had felt under her splayed fingertips as he'd bent her forward, how warm the water had been as it had stung her back and bottom. Mostly, though, she remembered how big he'd felt as he'd thrust into her from behind, how deeply he'd gone. She'd come so violently, her knees had buckled.

But after that?

"Yeah," he said softly.

She placed her hand against his chest, her fingers tingling for him. Yet as she pulled her gaze away from the bathroom, it accidentally skimmed over her walk-in closet. Darkness filled the back corners of the tiny room, the doors stood wide open, and the trail of shoes still led out of it. Her Somnambulist was getting stronger, controlling her longer and longer.

The chance she'd taken! She wasn't the only one vulnerable when she slept; he was even more at risk. For goodness sake, she'd almost run over that stranger with her car.

Derek's hand slid down to cup her hip. "What's wrong?"

Inhaling deeply, Shea looked at him.

Yet one look at his ruffled hair and sexy eyes and she

stopped herself. Why ruin the most erotic and sexually fulfilling day of her life? She had the perfect man in her bed: strong, smart, and sexy as hell. Why spoil this?

"Nothing's wrong."

"Are you sure?"

She trailed her fingers over his hard chest. "It's just waking up to find you here, in my bed. We seem to have skipped right over the dating part."

His dark eyes flared. "We'll date all you want."

He leaned close to kiss her again, rubbing slowly, taking the intimacy deeper by degrees. By the time his tongue swept across hers, her fingers were digging into his back.

"I can't get over how good you feel," he murmured, kissing his way under her chin. His hand stroked up her side to cup her breast. "Your skin is incredible. You know your business, Curie."

He said the name like an endearment. The inflection was so close to chéri, she looked up to see if he realized what he'd done.

He did.

"Phillip and I have worked very hard," she whispered.

"But you two never . . ."

She shook her head, blushing when she remembered how worked up that had made him. But Phillip wasn't ready for the world to know. Only she and Tamika knew the truth, and it made her uncomfortable that Derek had somehow found out. But that was what he did: he found out the truth, no matter how uncomfortable. An uneasy jitter ran down her spine. "We're just friends. *Best friends* ever since college."

"Don't worry. I won't out him." His thumb settled over her nipple and lingered. "I just don't think you realize the part you've been playing in keeping his secret. We could have been together long before now if I'd known."

Shea leveled a look on him. "You're no open book. The other day was the first time I realized you might even be interested. Other than work, I don't know much about you."

"I'm interested. What else do you want to know?"

"Are you serious?"

Shifting, he plumped the pillow under his head, then pulled her closer so she could lie against it, too. "I want to know about you, too."

It felt so strange, lying here naked with him, their skin brushing and their breaths mingling. The darkness in the room deepened, surrounding them and drawing the intimacy even closer. "Derek, you must have done a background check on me. That's . . . well, that's what you do."

He shook his head, the pillow rising and falling. "I made sure that Biodermatics was reputable, but I didn't go beyond that."

"Why not?"

"I wanted to hear it from you."

For some reason, that was the sexiest thing he'd said to her all day long. Unfortunately, it was also the most unsettling. If he hadn't looked into her background, then he really didn't know her at all. All he saw was the image she'd worked so hard to create, that of the polished professional. He didn't know about the events that had changed her life, why she worked so hard, or how badly darkness and fire scared her. "You like throwing me off balance, don't you?"

He smiled softly. "I'm beginning to find it one of my favorite things. Your turn now."

"For what?"

"To tell me anything and everything there is to know about Shea Caldwell." He snuggled against the pillow, looking as sexy and lazy as a tiger settling down for a nap. "Why biochemistry?"

The question surprised her, but it eased her as well. She suspected that was his intention. "It always clicked for me. Chemistry makes sense. Sometimes it's the only thing that does."

"Can't argue with you there." The look in his eyes told her he wasn't thinking about the kind of chemistry that required a periodic chart.

"There's so much good I can do with it," she said. "So many people I can help. I want to do more. I want to . . ."

She stopped. "What about you? Why corporate intelligence?"

"Because privacy is important to me, I believe in rules, and I'm very protective of what's mine."

She tried to think as his hand stroked over her skin. "But your brother is a newspaper editor."

"We're all different."

"There are more than two of you?"

He smiled. "I have more brothers than you can count, but no sisters."

She smiled with him. "Your poor mother."

"Don't feel sorry for her. She's a force to be reckoned with."

"What's her name?"

"Nyx."

Shea's fingers paused on his collarbone.

"What?" he asked.

She looked at him bemusedly. "I took a course in Greek mythology when I was an undergrad. Do you know the story of the Oneiroi, Derek?"

She felt the energy gather in him. It practically swirled around the bed. "I'm familiar with it," he said carefully.

The power coming off him was heady. Shea inhaled, absorbing it as her mind went back. "They were dark-winged daemons sent by the gods from a cavern on the shore of the ocean near Hades. When they appeared to humans, it was in their sleep. The Oneiroi could take whatever shape they wished, but true dreams emerged from a gate made of horn, while false dreams came from a gate made of ivory."

He cleared his throat. "Something like that."

"They were said to rule over sexual dreams most of all."

The room seemed to shrink, and Shea felt him everywhere they touched. If anyone ruled her sexual dreams, it was him. She cleared her throat. "Anyway, the mother of the Oneiroi was said to be Night, or Nyx."

He edged closer. "What do you think of all that?"

"The coincidence is fascinating. Derek Dream," she said, caught up in the mysticality of it, the sensuality. He probably thought she was silly. "I loved that class, particularly that myth."

"Myth," he repeated softly. His gaze dropped, yet his hand rubbed gentle circles at the small of her back. "Any reason for that?"

This time, she was the one who got careful. "I've just always been interested in stories that tried to explain things . . . the ones that predated the science that told the real truth. Folklore, I guess. Mrs. Lupescu used to tell me all kinds of fairy tales and legends."

"Mrs. Lupescu?"

Shea hesitated. He really did have a way of slipping past her defenses.

Or just storming her castle walls directly . . .

Discomfited, she pulled the sheet higher on her chest. "She was our neighbor in the mobile home park."

"Here in Solstice?"

"You really *didn't* do a background check on me."

"Tell me about this neighbor."

Shea twisted the sheet in her hand. That probably wasn't a good idea, especially now. Still, he'd be like a bulldog with a bone if she didn't give him something. "Mrs. Lupescu was this larger-than-life gypsy type. She'd tell me all kinds of fantastical stories when my dad was on the road, but she could get a little over the top."

"Your dad traveled a lot?"

"He was a truck driver. Well, actually, he's driving again. For Biodermatics." Her gaze dropped. "He . . . took a break for a while."

"Are you two close?"

"Very." Her eyes stung, and she rubbed them. "I think that's enough show and tell for today."

Derek's eyes narrowed, that familiar spark of curiosity flaring. Yet he tamped it down this time. "Maybe enough telling, but definitely not enough showing."

The hand at her back slid down her spine, sending her system into an uproar. After a day of making love, her body was beginning to know when he was serious.

And he was definitely serious about this.

His fingers kept going, all the way down to her tailbone. She tensed when they didn't stop there. Touching her gently but assuredly, his caress swept deep into the crevice between her rounded cheeks.

"So soft," he whispered against her lips.

Shea groaned as he touched her sensitive flesh, stroking and building a hunger she hadn't even known existed.

His fingers approached her pussy from behind. Two dipped into her, their entrance shallow and smooth. The moment he discovered how wet she was, his fingers pushed in farther, burrowing deep.

Shea arched in his embrace. He touched her like nobody else ever had, like he knew she was his.

"I can't believe this is happening between us," she whispered, smoothing her hand over his chest.

"It's happening." He brushed his lips against hers. "Touch me."

She felt his heart pounding against his rib cage, and her nipples stiffened in response. Looking into his eyes, she saw his need. He was as responsive to her as she was to him.

And, oh God, was she responding to him.

Her hips pushed down to meet each plunge of those thick, determined fingers. She ran her hands down his chest, over his belly, and across his six-pack abs. His pubic hair was rough and crinkly, but the heat of his cock was so unexpected, she paused.

A thrill went through her when he flinched.

"Don't stop," he groaned.

Shea fought for air as she rubbed her knuckles along his heavy staff from its base to its blunt tip. She found moisture there, his masculine to her feminine. She let it coat her fingers before wrapping them around the underside of his cock.

"Fuck," Derek panted, his fingers slamming into her almost roughly.

Shea let out a cry as her hips jumped in pleasure.

"Stroke it," he growled.

Eagerly, she pumped her hand up and down. He felt hot, hard, and silky. He was big, and her pussy squeezed at the thought of taking him again.

"Christ," he said, feeling her spasm.

She gasped when he suddenly pulled his fingers out of her. The loss left her aching, but he caught the back of her thigh and pulled her leg over his hip.

"Now."

She directed his erection to where she needed it the most, and the moment the head dipped into her notch, he pushed into her.

Her breath caught in her lungs.

"Okay?" he asked, his hand catching her by the lower back.

She lifted her leg higher, over his waist. "I love the way you feel."

She felt his muscles clench, and then he was filling her again. His thick cock drove slowly up into her, stretching long unused muscles, until he was seated all the way inside her.

Her leg wrapped snugly around his hip, and her arms held him close. His whiskers scraped against her cheek as he took a long, slow breath.

"I'm glad we didn't stop to date first. I don't think I could have waited."

"Me, either."

Their mouths met as he began to thrust into her slowly, sexily. Shea found his rhythm and met him stroke for stroke. Their bodies sealed tightly, her breasts plumping against his chest. Their combined body temperature heated the dark air around them, and the night became sultry.

They kept it slow, until their skin slickened, their bodies were straining, and neither of them could stand it any longer.

"Ah!" Shea cried when Derek thrust a little firmer, a little faster.

She looked into his dark eyes and saw pure pleasure.

"Yes," she agreed.

His thrusts became more urgent, quicker and rougher. She took him greedily, and the rhythm soon had the headboard knocking against the wall.

"Oh, God. Derek!"

Shea arched as her orgasm hit her hard. The waves just kept coming over her as the headboard knocked and banged. Derek buried his head into the curve of her neck as he fucked her right through it. When his release came, his shout of completion was even sexier.

His weight finally came down against her and his hips pinned her in place. Their skin clung as they both struggled to catch their breaths.

Slowly, he pulled back. His hand was a bit unsteady as he brushed her hair back from her face. Shea felt shaky, too.

His weight felt good against her. *Right*. The darkness around them was complete; night had fallen. It was the first time in years she'd felt comfortable in it, safe. Yet she could feel sleep sneaking up on her again, coiled and ready to pounce.

Anxiety hummed over her skin.

She looked into Derek's fathomless eyes. She didn't want to hurt his feelings. She didn't want to jeopardize the relationship they'd just started, either.

But all of that took a backseat to protecting him.

"It's getting late," she said gently.

His brow furrowed. "So?"

"So . . . tomorrow is a workday. I'm sure you want to get an early start."

"I'd rather sleep in with you."

She glanced over his shoulder and shivered when she saw the closet gaping like a huge, dark mouth. "You said just for the day. . . ."

"Are you asking me to leave?"

She smiled sadly. "I've loved being with you today, Derek. I really have, but . . . I think it's time you should go."

The mist started collecting in the corner of the room. Particles gathered, shifting as the form took shape. Yet even assembled, the being was amorphous. Free-flowing. The Somnambulist entered his She-a's room carefully, putting out feelers as he went, sniffing the air. . . .

The scent of Wreaker filled his brain, scrambling his thoughts. It was the most feared scent for his kind, a killing scent.

Yet the room was empty, save for his beloved.

His pretty, pretty girl.

She lay on the bed, her blond hair flowing around her shoulders. Her sweet toes peeked out from under the rumpled covers, and he licked his lips. She was too tempting for him to leave, even with the threat of danger lurking.

He edged toward her, aching to be with her again. He wanted her power, craved her ability for physical touch. His toes fluttered in anticipation as he crept forward, but he stayed on guard. The Wreaker had left, but his She-a wasn't dreaming.

The creature's eyes narrowed.

What was a Wreaker doing here if not bestowing dreams?

Possessiveness heated him from the inside out. His She-a was *his*. His to be with, his to enjoy. Reaching out, he stroked his clawlike fingers over her shoulder. He watched as they disappeared into her body and wished he could feel the resiliency of her skin.

A growl rose up from his thin chest.

Something was wrong. *Again.*

Her arm was like a bag of sand, heavy and dead. For nights, it had been like this. Ever since they'd taken that drive in her car, she'd been fighting him.

A hiss left his lips. Was the Wreaker responsible for this?

The creature bent down so near that her breaths pushed right through him. He peered at her eyelids, but they were smooth and still. Dreams weren't what held her down.

What had the Oneiroi done to her?

"Arggggh!" With a lurch, he powered himself up over her. He hovered for a moment, then let himself slowly drop. He filled her up from head to toe, letting his essence congregate.

She felt heavy and cloudy, and cobwebs filled her head. Frustration had his particles shaking. Why did he have to work so hard to get her to respond to his commands? Why was she keeping her delicious, wonderful power from him? After all he'd done for her, how dare she treat him this way?

He tried to sit her up, but couldn't. Snarling, he tried to move her head. Open her eyes. Lift a finger. Wiggle her toes.

Panting, he stared at the backs of her eyelids. He needed to focus. It was how he'd taken charge of her last night, when he'd tried to show her that the face in the window was back. There it had been, hateful eyes glaring. He'd shown it to her, and he'd left a trail to remind her, setting out all her pretty, colorful shoes.

He licked his lips, remembering how it had felt to be corporeal for that long, how sumptuous it had been. He wanted that control back.

Closing his eyes, he held on to his anger. He let it feed him, hone his concentration. The moment he did, he realized her body felt different. Something had changed. It wasn't only heavy and cloudy, it was hot and . . . tickly. Sensitive.

"Hmm," he hummed. What was this?

Trapped as he was, he could sense every inch of her, and beneath the weighted fog he detected something. Something pulsing with energy. The pink bumps on her chest . . . They were all pointy and tingly. And that spot between her legs felt *awake*.

This was new.

He went very still, concentrating on that tender spot. Was that slickness? Between her thighs? He tried to rub her legs together, but she remained frozen in place.

"Aarrrgggh," he cried in frustration.

There was a secret here, a power that he craved.

He had to find a way to tap into it.

He shook his head inside She-a's, trying to clear out the cobwebs that tangled up her brain. "Let me in!"

He needed to blast through those sticky webs, find a way to connect with her. He focused all his concentration downward, and was surprised when those pink nubs throbbed and that *awake* spot squeezed.

He tried it again, and those achy spots on her body sang. So did he. He sent the impulses down over and over again, until—

Her toes wiggled along with his.

He gurgled deep in his throat. He loved her toes!

Soon he had her feet.

Excitement made him work harder. If he could wiggle her toes, could he wiggle her fingers? He sent his concentration through her and felt the pink bumps on her chest tighten almost painfully.

Oh, this was working better than anything else. He flicked her fingers back and forth, feeling the circulation build. He circled her wrists and bent her arms at the elbows.

Finally, he managed to lift her head.

Those pink tips were pointing so high into the air, they looked as if they were trying to poke right through her clothes. Curious, he used her hand to touch. The blue material was slick, soft, and slippery.

"Oooh," he crooned. He liked that.

"Ah!" he hissed when her fingertips bumped up against that pointy tip. He liked *that* better, and so did she. He pressed the soft point again, and electricity coursed straight down to that magic spot between her legs.

The sensation made them both shudder.

Oh, the power. It was luscious and potent. He had to have it. He needed *more*!

Using her fingers, he squeezed and plucked at the pink nub, feeling the power lash through them both. Wanting more, he let her pinch and twist it.

With a cry of pleasure, her body lifted right off the bed.

The Somnambulist stopped, stunned.

She'd done that, not him.

Using her hands, he pushed them under the slippery material and excitedly caught both the full mounds. She squeezed them, pinched them, and rolled them. The pink bumps beaded up until they were tiny and hard. The power was so scintillating, he could hardly stand it.

An idea flashed inside his head, a brilliant idea. If it felt good touching her there . . .

He had both her hands diving down when warning signs suddenly clanged in his head. He jerked her head up. Nostrils flaring, he took a quick whiff.

"Wreaker!"

Not now!

The creature's particles instinctively jumped, trying to scatter. The room was taking on a different charge, and a shimmering had appeared on the opposite side of the bed.

Fear warred with pleasure. Wants clashed with instinct. Knowing he couldn't stay, the Somnambulist lurched out of his hostess's willing body. The quick disconnect was painful, ripping.

Looking at the bed with regret, he started to disperse. He hated to leave just as they were on the verge of something exciting. "I'll be back for you, my pretty girl," he promised.

Oh yes, he'd be back for her soon.

Real, real soon.

Eight

She'd made him leave. Just asked him to go. Any way you put it, Derek was pissed.

He was also worried as hell.

The day had been perfect—or so he'd thought. He'd gotten closer to Shea than he'd ever believed possible, and she'd wanted to be with him, too. Her body warmed when he touched her; her eyes softened. She trusted him physically; that was clear.

But it didn't go beyond that.

Punching his pillow, he tried to get more comfortable. Something had made her want him out of the house, but he didn't think it was anything he'd done. She'd seemed troubled and sad as she'd closed the door behind him. The look in her eyes had just about killed him. Why would she want to be alone at night? If someone *was* threatening her, wouldn't she have asked him to stay?

None of it made sense.

Rolling onto his back, he tried to relax. He'd gone along with her request only because he could go right back. And he would, if he could just get to sleep.

He rested his wrist against his forehead as he stared up at the ceiling. Insomnia wasn't usually a problem for Dream Wreakers; they slept differently from humans. Tonight, though, he was too worked up to get into the state of relaxation he needed, the one that put his physical body into stasis and let his spirit fly.

Letting out a deep breath, he forced his muscles to relax. Trying to stop his brain never worked. Instead, he squeezed his fists, then let the tension flow out of his fingertips. He did the same with his toes. He worked his way through his body until, finally, he concentrated on simply inhaling and exhaling. Inhaling and exhaling.

Suddenly he was there, detached from the human world. His spirit split from his sleeping earthly form, and he astral projected it into the dream realm.

Calls from his charges immediately hit his ears.

"Shit." He'd forgotten about them.

For a long, conflicted moment, duty pulled at him. He'd never ignored his responsibilities before, but pushing his guilt away, he headed straight for Shea's condo. He'd get to the others later. He'd be worthless to them until he figured out what was going on with her. The moment he sensed her brain wave pattern, the rest of the din faded into the background. He materialized in her bedroom, concentrating solely on her.

That mistake could have meant his end: he wasn't the only one there.

Zane spun toward him, hands lifted. His brown eyes were fierce, and his jaw was like granite. Derek automatically stepped back into a fighting position.

"Damn it, Derek," Zane said, gritting his teeth when he recognized him.

Whirling back around, he faced the bed. Shea slumbered on, beautiful and unaware. Yet every muscle in Zane's body was tense as he scanned the room.

Derek quickly went on the alert and turned the other way, guarding his brother's back. Concentrating, he tried to pick up on whatever Zane was feeling and caught it immediately. The vibrating hum was strange and *close*. It started in his hands and traveled to his chest. It echoed there, faint but sinister.

And it wasn't fading.

"Do you feel that?" Zane asked.

"I feel it." Derek's hands came up, ready for an onslaught. "*Find it.*"

The Somnambulist hadn't gone far.

He couldn't, not after what he'd just found.

Feeling greedy and territorial, he hovered outside the windows of his She-a's home. Awful Wreakers. They might think they owned her, but they didn't. He'd found a way past the foggy haze they'd put inside her head. But what were they doing back here? And why two of them?

Taking care not to get caught, he let his form stretch so it could barely be seen. Barely be detected. He peeked inside, but one of the big Wreakers turned sharply and his hands came up. The creature cringed back, elongating and stretching till he nearly came apart. Deadly hands, those were. Hands of sizzle and burn.

"You sense something?" the first Wreaker asked.

A growl rumbled up inside the creature, making his particles quiver in outrage. That was the one who'd chased him out of his beloved's room, out of her very body. Just a few more minutes with her, and he would have found something momentous. He knew it!

The scary Dream Wreaker didn't answer. His attention focused on the window, and, for a split second, the Somnambulist's particles froze in place. It took everything he had not to shriek. The Wreaker's eyes burned and gleamed. He moved closer to the window, and the Somnambulist trembled in fear.

He knew he should disperse. One Wreaker was dangerous; two were deadly. Moving carefully, the creature shifted to the next window. His gaze raked over his lovely's blond hair and rounded shoulders.

Another host wouldn't suit him. He was old, ancient for his kind. With age came a need for more energy. Easy targets like children couldn't give him the juice he needed. His She-a was an adult now, too—and he'd just found a power source in her so vast, he could survive without her for nights.

Or even better, stay with her longer and longer. With that kind of power, he might even be able to be with her all night.

And she needed that.

Anger flared inside him when he remembered the face in the window, that figure in black. His beloved hadn't known anyone was peeking inside her home night after night, but *he* had. Without him, she never would have been able to chase the nasty bugger away.

No, no. The Wreakers couldn't protect her like he could. *They couldn't have her.*

The Somnambulist watched his enemies. They wanted to play hide-and-seek? He was an expert. For years, he'd slipped out of their reach. Unfortunately, others hadn't been so lucky. He'd heard what they did to his kind.

Sizzle, sizzle. Regular or extra crispy?

It was a risk he was willing to take.

Knowing he'd pushed his luck far enough for tonight, though, he let himself vaporize and disappear.

But he'd be back.

The Dream Wreaker with the tough eyes couldn't be here all the time. He had other sleepers to attend to.

Fortunately, Somnambulists only needed one.

"I don't feel it anymore," Zane said.

"It's gone."

Zane relaxed from the defensive posture he'd taken. Still, he was on guard. "What was it?"

Derek wished to God he knew. The vibration had been odd, familiar yet not. It was so faint, though, he couldn't be sure about anything—other than a night creature had been nearby.

That was bad enough.

He peered outside the window for any signs. Dark clouds were stamped against the moon. The air was heavy with humidity, but nothing moved. The leaves hung limp on tree branches, and the grass beaded up with moisture.

A bad feeling niggled at him. Turning back to the bed, his gaze immediately went to Shea. She was sleeping soundly; he could feel the delta waves from where he stood. She was in stage four, ready to be led up into REM sleep.

It wasn't a good sign. Too many night creatures liked to strike early in the night before he and his brothers made their first appearance.

"I felt it as soon as I manifested," Zane said. "But then you appeared, and I lost the trace. What the hell are you doing here, Derek? She's my charge."

"I know."

"But you still think I'm messing with her dreams?" His brother's jaw hardened. Moving faster than his lackadaisical reputation indicated, he came across the room and got in Derek's face. "I know you're The Machine, and I'm The Screwup. That's the way everybody likes it, clean and simple. But I take care of her, Derek. No matter what label you throw on me, I'm good at what I do. Damn good."

"I know that, too." Derek rolled his shoulders. *He* was the one who wasn't doing his job tonight, yet he identified with his brother's anger. He was sick of being labeled, and he wasn't an unfeeling robot. "This isn't about you. It's about me."

"You think you're better than I am?"

"No. I think I couldn't stay away—not even when she asked."

Zane blinked and took a step back. He glanced toward the bed and then back again. "Did things not go well between you two?"

Derek glared at him. What had happened between him and Shea was private, yet just as he was about to inform Zane of that, he realized his brother sounded disappointed. Disappointed and kind of sympathetic.

Hell, was he that pathetic?

"Hey, I'm not implying anything," Zane said, lifting his hands. "I expected you to be here—but in that bed with her, not floating in the dream realm with me."

Derek looked at the empty space at Shea's side. "Yeah. Me, too."

"So . . . what happened?"

Derek shifted uncomfortably. "She kicked me out."

"She did *not*." Zane tried to hold back, but that just wasn't the kind of guy he was. "Are you serious? What did you do? You can't tell me the sex wasn't good."

He gestured about the room. Pillows, bedding, and shoes were strewn everywhere. Lotions had been scattered across the dressing table, and two damp towels were draped over the side of the tub in the master bath.

Derek stiffened, but proof was proof. "We were . . . compatible. She just didn't want to sleep with me. Now I think I understand why."

They both looked to the bed uneasily. "When she said sleep, she meant *sleep*," he added.

"She knows something's after her." Moving instinctively back to her side, Zane stood guard. If anything was out there stalking her in the night, he was the one bound to protect her.

But God, Derek wanted to be in his place.

He rubbed the back of his neck. He should have

pressed her harder. She'd told him that she hadn't been sleeping well; she just hadn't let him know how bad it was. With night creatures lurking, it had to be bad. He swore underneath his breath. His instincts had been right the first time, yet he'd let himself get distracted with that trespasser. Although that was a bad scene, too.

What the hell was going on?

He kicked a pillow at his feet. He needed to think with the head on his shoulders, not the one that seemed to pop to attention whenever she walked in the room.

"Check the dresser." Turning, he quickly went into the bathroom. A night-light glowed steadily. "Is this always on?"

"She's afraid of the dark."

"Damn," Derek muttered. The darkness was where he was most comfortable. It was his home, his retreat.

His spine stiffened. The most telling sign of all sat on the counter beside the sink. "Sleeping pills."

"Prescription?"

"Over-the-counter." Feeling tense and ready to pop, Derek leaned his arm against the doorjamb and stared hard at the bed. Asleep, Shea looked sweet and vulnerable. Her lips were parted as if awaiting a kiss. She'd put that ice-blue nightie back on, but the sheet had drifted low across her breasts. She'd been fighting this scourge on her own, and fighting hard. If only he'd known . . . If only Zane had known . . .

But they hadn't, and now they had to play catch-up.

"She's a scientist," Derek said flatly. "She doesn't

know she's a target. In her mind, she thinks she has a parasomnia, a sleep disorder."

"Yeah, but which one?"

The vibration seemed to reappear in Derek's hands, and he had to flex his fingers to shake it. The hum had been low and powerful, like a big, bass amplifier. Frustration filled him when he still couldn't place it. "How does she normally sleep? What's a typical night like?"

Zane shrugged. "She's a lot like you. When it comes to sleep, she has very strict routines. She goes to bed at the same time every night, and she takes dreams easily. In the past few weeks, though, something's changed. I don't sense her until late."

Derek paused. He wasn't sensing Tamika until the wee hours of the night, either.

"It could be due to her work," Zane cautioned. "I've found her sleeping over her papers or with a book falling out of her hand."

"She works too hard." Derek frowned. "How have her dreams been? Any more nightmares?"

"Other than the wet ones?"

He hadn't known he could growl.

Zane's lips twitched. "Sorry."

His brother ruffled his mop of hair. "She has really unique dreams," he confided. "She dreams in equations, chemical formulas, and reactions. I'll find her walking all over a molecule, trying to find where to attach a carbon element. She's brilliant," Zane said quietly. "I can't make heads or tails of what she's thinking, but it's impressive."

"I'm surprised you know what a molecule looks like."

"I'm not a complete idiot."

"No, you just play one sometimes." Derek let out a long breath. Bantering with Zane made him feel better, like things were on a steadier keel than they really were.

"What else?" he asked. He needed to know more if he was going to help her.

"She's terrified of fire."

Derek looked up sharply.

"Most of her nightmares center on it," his brother said.

The Bunsen burner. He remembered the way she'd stopped to double-check that it was off; she'd seemed almost obsessive about it.

"But she loves Baby Ruth candy bars," Zane offered. "If you want to find a way back into her bed, that might be a good way to sweeten her up."

"But she's a Mets fan," Derek said absently.

"A Mets fan who craves a chocolate bar named after the biggest Yankee ever," Zane said. "That's why it's a secret."

She had a lot of secrets. Too many.

Derek closed his eyes. So did he.

He could help her with this, but how could he explain that to her? How could he tell a top-notch biochemist that he wasn't quite human? That he was a Dream Wreaker who traveled through another realm at night to bestow dreams? She might like the fantasy, but she'd never accept the reality. At best, she'd think he was mocking her.

At worst, she'd think he was insane.

"Go ahead," Zane said.

Derek looked up. "What?"

"Take a swing at me. You've got every right."

"What are you talking about?"

Guilt rippled across his brother's boyish face, but he stood a little straighter. "I screwed up. I obviously let something get by me."

"Ah, hell. So did I." Derek pushed himself away from the wall. "I missed it, too."

Moving automatically to the bed, Derek reached for Shea's forehead. The best way to help her was to get her back into a normal sleep cycle, starting with REM sleep. As his fingers brushed over her brow, though, he remembered his place and made himself take a step back. "Take care of her."

Zane looked at him sharply. "Are you sure?"

"She's yours."

"My *charge* maybe, but you should take over with her now."

The unexpected offer made Derek's pulse jump.

Still, he looked at his little brother. Really looked. "I trust you, Zane. I might not like your methods sometimes. The way you play around in people's heads drives me nuts—but it also makes me realize how good you are at this."

"But you want her."

"Yeah, I do."

"So take her."

Just like that. Take her.

Zane lived by impulse, but it was harder for Derek. He wanted to grab the opportunity with both hands, yet there was more to consider. Would it put him too close? And how would it affect his relationship with his brother? For all his nonchalant attitude, Zane had been Shea's Dream Wreaker for a long time. If he really believed Derek didn't think he was good enough for her . . .

Zane cleared his throat, obviously uncomfortable at the silence. "I've got to warn you, though, it's going to cost you."

Derek braced himself. That cocky look was back in his brother's eyes. "Cost me how?" he asked carefully.

"You'll have to trade me someone for her. One hottie for another." Zane's gaze slid over Shea's form. It was soft and protective, yet he smiled mischievously. "A woman like this? Hell, you might have to give me two."

Derek had an uncanny suspicion that he was being let off the hook.

And his brother had a point. He really couldn't take on Shea, knowing she had sleep issues, without giving somebody up. He might not have the time to treat them all equally—and he knew that she was going to get his best.

"Somebody sexy," Zane prodded. "Somebody smokin'."

An idea hit Derek, and it was perfect. "Tamika Hendricks."

"Really?" Zane said, perking up. "What's she look like?"

Derek rounded the bed, deadly serious about this. It would kill two birds with one stone. "She works with Shea, and she's been calling for me late, too. She'll take dreams when I give them to her, but finding her asleep has been a problem. When I saw her the other day, she looked troubled."

His brother's humor left fast. "Do you think there's a connection?"

"I don't know. Maybe." Either way, Derek didn't like it. "You know what this thing feels like now. You can be on watch for it. I'd do it, but—"

"But you'd rather be here." Zane planted his hands on his hips, yet one eyebrow cocked. "Is she good looking?"

Derek felt the familiar desire to knock his brother upside the head—and it made him feel so much better about things. "She's unbelievably hot. Long, lean, runner's legs. High, perky breasts. And she can have some pretty kinky dreams."

"You had me at the legs."

"It's a deal then. Tamika's yours, and Shea's mine."

Together, they looked at the beautiful blonde on the bed.

Unexpectedly, Zane cuffed him upside the shoulder. "Machine Man, I think you might have finally met your match."

Nine

Shea didn't want to throw Derek out of her bed ever again.

She'd hated the look on his face as he'd stood on her front stoop under the moonlight. He hadn't complained or argued; he'd simply kissed the daylights out of her before saying goodnight. Yet she'd seen the look in his eyes. He'd been disappointed—and worried. She knew that glint, and she was tired of being responsible for it.

She was tired of so many things: being scared, being out of control, and simply being vulnerable. She was determined to get her life back, and she'd just taken the first step.

Lifting the brown plastic bottle up to the sunlight, she gave it a jiggle. The sleeping pills inside rattled. She hoped this prescription medication worked better than the over-the-counter stuff. As far as she could tell she hadn't sleepwalked last night, but she had a strange, uneasy feeling she just couldn't shake. Her Somnambulist might not have wandered with her last night, but it had visited.

The hair at the back of her neck rose. How was it going to react to *this?*

She shoved the pills into her purse and got out of her car. She needed to stop thinking like that. She had a sleep disorder; a sleep arousal disorder, to be precise. Her doctor had explained that she was coming too close to wakefulness as she progressed through the sleep stages. There was a scientific, clinical explanation for what had been happening to her. She was *not* a victim of some long-ago childhood monster.

Even though she still might feel like it.

Lifting her chin, she opened the front door of Bioder-matics and stepped inside. As serious as her personal problems were, she had others to deal with here.

Tamika's head popped up when she heard the *whoosh* of the door's piston, and she quickly shoved something in her desk drawer. Their newest employee, however, was engrossed in something. Walking crisply, Shea headed over to the desk that had been set up across from Tamika's main reception area. "Good morning, Lynette. Welcome to Biodermatics."

The woman looked up from the list of ingredients she was reading on the label of their wrinkle cream. "Oh, Dr. Caldwell!"

She quickly stood and tugged at the hem of her sweater, trying to get the material to smooth over her hips. "My stepmother used to love that stuff."

Shea smiled. "Feel free to take some samples."

Lynette's eyes widened, and she quickly pushed the bottle away. "Oh, no. I mean . . . I couldn't."

"Of course you can. You work here now."

"And I'm so happy to be here. Thank you for giving me this opportunity."

"We're glad to have you. We've needed more help around here for a while."

Lynette nodded solemnly. "I'm willing to contribute wherever I can. With my chemistry background, I'm sure you'll find me useful. I could even help out in the lab if you'd like."

Shea blinked in surprise. "Let's start with the front office work first."

"Oh, of course. I didn't mean anything."

"I appreciate your enthusiasm. Has anyone shown you around yet?"

"Phillip did." The phone on Lynette's desk started to ring. "He showed me the facilities and introduced me to everyone who was here. Do you always come in this late?"

Shea was taken aback. "I had an appointment. Usually I'm one of the first ones here."

Lynette's forehead furrowed. "But I was just acquainting myself with the scheduling system, and I didn't see anything on there for you."

"Ahem," Tamika said loudly. "She doesn't have to clear her schedule with us; she's the company *president*. And if you're not too busy, that's Phillip's line."

"Oh! That's me." Lynette tilted her head sheepishly. "I'm not used to answering phones for other people."

"Yet," Tamika said succinctly.

Shea glanced her assistant's way. Tamika rolled her

eyes and lifted up two messages. Shea's heart jumped. Were any of them from Derek?

"What am I, chopped liver?" her assistant grunted. She played keep-away with the messages when Shea reached for them. "You walked by without even saying hello."

"Hello, Tamika. Good morning." One look at her friend and Shea could see that she'd gotten up on the wrong side of the bed. She could sympathize. Discreetly, she nodded her head to the side. "How's she doing?"

"Ms. I've-got-a-background-in-chemistry?"

Inwardly, Shea sighed. "What's wrong?"

With a flourish, Tamika rolled back her chair and crossed her arms over her chest. "She's annoying, that's what wrong. She's just such an eager beaver—and I do not mean that in the good, kinky way."

"Give her a chance. She's excited about having a new job."

Tamika leaned closer. "I don't like her."

The angry hiss startled Shea. Usually her assistant was outgoing and effervescent, yet that sunny personality had recently faded. More and more she was becoming snippy and guarded, definitely short-tempered. "Are you okay?" she asked.

"I'm fine."

Fine wasn't usually displayed with a scowl and lowered eyebrows.

"Tired," Tamika admitted, shuffling papers on her desk.

"I'm counting on you to help train her," Shea said.

Her assistant's pretty dark skin flushed. Nodding, she handed over the messages.

Shea looked through them quickly and was disappointed when she didn't see Derek's name. Worriedly, she flicked the corners of the slips until the writing blurred.

He'd been frustrated when he'd left, but was he angry with her? Her teeth settled into her lower lip. As wonderful as yesterday had been, it had all been so sudden. And with her sleep problems, she wasn't ready to let him spend the night. It was going to be days before she was fully convinced that the new sleeping pills were the answer to her problems.

"There you are," Phillip said, stepping into the open doorway of his office. He looked crisp and professional in his deep blue shirt and red tie. "We need to iron out the production schedule. Remember?"

Shea's shoulders slumped. Whatever happened to tackling one problem at a time? "Give me a minute. I'll be right there."

Yet as she headed to her office, the production schedule was the last thing on her mind. Every brush of her skirt against her thighs brought back memories of Derek's hands on her. Her lips were swollen under her lipstick, and her nipples were sensitive against her bra. None of that compared, though, to how she felt between her legs.

Her body felt as if it had just been jump-started, and she didn't know how to handle it.

Knowing that Phillip would come by soon, she set

down her briefcase and stashed her purse. She grabbed her notebook, but couldn't find her favorite pen. She searched for it, but finally gave up and pulled another out of the drawer. Pushing her decidedly unprofessional thoughts out of her mind, she headed to the hallway. Her footsteps slowed when she glanced down.

"Darn it." She'd picked up her lab book, not her business notebook.

She backtracked to her desk, where she found her business notes sitting atop the latest issue of the *Journal of Dermatological Science*. It made her frown. That was the research-related pile. She was very organized, especially when it came to separating the two aspects of her job. Still, she had been harried recently.

But not enough to leave her chair pulled out and sitting at a cockeyed angle.

She took an uneasy step backward. Tucking chairs away was an ingrained habit of a sleepwalker. She did it unconsciously, but she also did it habitually. Her gaze went to the window, where the Dumpster sat in clear view.

This was not how she'd left things. Somebody had been at her desk.

She nabbed her lab book and backed away. Turning on her heel, she hurried to her partner's office.

"Phillip, has anyone—"

Lynette suddenly appeared in the doorway. "Do you need me to take notes?"

Shea's nerves nearly snapped. Drawing into herself, she stiffly moved to the back corner of the room. Phillip glanced at her quickly. Moving between her and their overeager staff member, he smiled soothingly. "We're really not that kind of an office. Not enough staff, not enough airs."

Lynette looked chastened. Over her shoulder, Shea could see Tamika smiling smugly.

"Tell you what." Phillip reached into his pocket and pulled out his keys. "If you could load my car with those samples in the conference room, I'd appreciate it."

Lynette's lips twisted. "The moisturizer or the eye cream?"

"Both of them, and organize them, please."

She sighed. "Yes, sir."

She left, and Phillip quickly closed the door after her. "What's wrong?"

"Has anyone been in my office today?" Shea asked.

"I don't know. It's been a busy morning. Why?"

She put her notebooks down on his desk. They tracked all the blood, sweat, and tears that had gone into making Biodermatics the profitable company that it was. Worriedly, she traced the edge of her lab book's leather cover. "Did you check our main offices the night I saw that trespasser on the property?"

"Yes, and this building was locked up tight."

"And our security system hasn't shown any unusual entries?"

Her partner's brow furrowed. "Don't you think Derek would have been all over that?"

"Right," she said softly.

Phillip stepped closer. "Let me try again. What's wrong?"

Shea let out a shaky breath. She had an eerie feeling that her Somnambulist had come calling last night, but could it have actually brought her over here, gotten inside the building, done *whatever*, and returned her home to her bed without her knowing? She raked a hand through her hair. "Somebody was in my things."

Her partner's face tightened. "Are you certain?"

"It was subtle, but things had been moved. Little things might be missing. You know how you just *know*?"

Phillip yanked the phone out of its base and began jabbing at the speed dial. "Derek was right. Someone is after our company secrets."

Shea caught the phone and her partner's hand in both of hers. "Wait."

"He has to know; it's what we pay him for."

"Just stop." His grip loosened, and she put the cordless phone back into its base. "We need to look at the check-ins, see who came in over the weekend."

Derek had set up a security system that required all employees to swipe their ID cards to enter during off-hours.

"Good idea." Phillip came around her, sat in his chair, opened up the computer program, and began to type in rapid hunt-and-pecks.

"See if I logged in," Shea said.

His shoulders hitched. "Did somebody steal your card?"

"Not in the way you think."

It took a moment, but when he swiveled toward her, understanding was in his eyes. "Honey, you couldn't have sleepwalked all the way over here. There's no way."

Shea felt her throat thicken. She'd done a lot of things without knowing, things she'd never even told Phillip about. "It's not out of the realm of possibility. My doctor warned me just today that there have been cases of people having sex with strangers or even committing murder while they were asleep. I've already driven my car. . . . Just look, okay?"

Phillip's attention returned to their security log. Neither of them realized they were holding their breaths until he let out a long sigh. "The only person to check into the main office this weekend was me, and I didn't touch your things."

Then the only other option was that somebody had snooped around her office this morning.

Hesitantly, they both looked toward the door.

"No," she said. She trusted their employees. "Maybe it was just Bonita."

Phillip shook his head. "She's always very careful not to disturb things when she cleans my office. What was missing?"

"Just a pen and perhaps an envelope I scribbled some formulae on. I didn't see it." Shea pinched the bridge of her nose. "Maybe I'm making a mountain out of a molehill. Somebody probably just knocked the things off my desk and put them back in the wrong place."

"The same somebody who dressed like a ninja to go through our trash the other night?" Phillip reached again for the phone. "I'm calling Derek."

"No!" Shea flushed when her partner looked at her sharply. "I'll go see him. I . . . I need to talk to him anyway."

Phillip's eyebrows rose.

"He came over this weekend," she confessed.

"And?"

She shrugged uncomfortably.

"If you don't give me more information than that, I'm going to hide all your pipettes. What happened? Did he do something you didn't want to do? Because I don't care how big and muscle-bound he is; if he hurt you, I'll rip his Adam's apple out and feed it to him."

As implausible as the picture was, her friend's protectiveness was touching.

"It wasn't like that. Derek was . . . perfect." Shea took a bracing breath. "But I had to send him home. I had no other choice."

"You sent him home?" Phillip looked at her as if she were insane. "What were you thinking?"

"I was thinking that I'm a sleepwalker who rams her car at people."

Her partner let out a strangled sound. "Just tell him you've got a sleep disorder!"

"*Think* about it. Derek is a fixer: he solves problems and protects things. But he's not a doctor or a therapist. I can't have him around, not when I'm sleeping. It's too dangerous for both of us."

"Come on, Shea. I know you want him. Don't break the guy's heart—or your own."

She blinked, stunned. Was Derek's heart really in the game?

Just the idea had her own heart pounding faster.

"Go see him. Tell him the truth."

The idea was almost tempting, until she noticed how protectively her hand sat on her notebooks. Suddenly, all she could think about was the figure in black and the angry way it had stood over her car. If that person had put his hands on her research . . . She shook her head, feeling sick. "He needs to know about this more. He's got to find whoever is doing this and stop them *now*."

"Damn," Derek said under his breath. The soft tone didn't take away the vehemence. He stared at the computer screen, hating what he was reading, but unable to stop.

Paging down, he continued reading the newspaper article he'd found in the *Sentinel* archives. He'd been at this all morning and had learned a lot about Shea. He'd read about her schooling and the accolades she'd received as a young researcher at the university. The business section had boasted the successes of her start-up company, but this story went further back—back to the time she was that little girl in the trailer park.

What he was reading made it hard to breathe.

Unwillingly, he stared at the black-and-white photograph that showed the melted, buckled wad of metal that had once been her home. Bracing himself, he continued reading the write-up. Unknown source. One injury. Total loss. Firefighters had originally been unable to locate the young girl who lived in the trailer, but she'd eventually been discovered outside the scene.

Thank God.

He ran his hand across his face. No wonder her nightmares were about fire.

Guiltily, he looked at the file he'd created. He didn't like the tactics he'd had to take, but after his discussion with Zane he'd had to know more. Shea *had* given him tacit approval; she'd told him she'd expected him to do a background check on her.

She'd just seemed happy that he hadn't.

His pen bounced when he tossed it on the desk. There was no way around it. He was a snake in the grass.

He could justify it every which way to Sunday, but she'd gotten into his head and under his skin. He wanted to know everything there was to know about her. He wanted to know her favorite colors, the breakthroughs she was making in her laboratory, the sexual positions that got her off. . . .

And why she was taking those goddamned sleeping pills.

His fingers flexed. If only he could identify that strange vibration he'd felt in her bedroom. It had just been a tingling, a rattling on the edge of his senses. There were too many night creatures that could be haunting her, taunting her.

Possessiveness roared up inside him. They wouldn't

be having their way with her much longer—not once he caught them.

But catching them was the problem.

Derek gave the computer mouse a shove. Like a good, dependable Dream Wreaker, he'd completed his rounds last night, including taking Zane to Tamika. She'd only been in the first stage of the sleep cycle, just barely falling asleep. It left him uncertain. Had he missed something? Was there more he could be doing?

A tap at the door made him look up. "Come in," he called, automatically closing the manila file folder.

The door opened, but instead of Ellen's dark head, he saw the shine of natural blond. He was on his feet before he remembered the information he still had pulled up on his computer. Feeling caught in the act, he abruptly closed the screen. "Shea, come in."

She closed the door behind her. "I need to talk to you."

She was polished and reserved again in her tidy blue suit. Too bad all he could think of was ripping it off her. Yet there was an edginess to her, an aggression she couldn't hide. "Is this business or pleasure?"

"Business." Her steps paused. "I might have more information about that prowler."

Derek snapped to attention fast. Rounding his desk, he directed her to the sofa. "Sit down."

She eyed the leather couch warily and moved toward his desk instead. His gaze flashed worriedly to the file. "What happened?" he asked.

She put her briefcase on the floor by a chair and

turned to pace. "Somebody has been looking around my office."

"*Your office?*" He had enough security features in place that that shouldn't happen.

"My business notebook and my lab book were switched. Some notes are missing, and my office wasn't as I left it." She wrapped her arms around her waist, outrage practically radiating from her. "I think somebody went through my things."

"No alarms were set off recently." He turned toward his computer. "Let me check the card swipes."

"Phillip already did that. He didn't notice anything out of the ordinary."

"Was someone careless with their ID?"

She stopped pacing for a moment. "Either that, or they had permission to be there."

Their gazes locked. She suspected one of her own.

"What about your lab?" he asked, his voice going hard.

"It seemed undisturbed."

"What about your employees? Have you noticed any unusual behavior lately? Have attendance habits changed? Is anyone having financial problems that might make him susceptible to others' interests?"

She paled visibly and started pacing again, her movements anxious and stiff. "I didn't really believe you when you said somebody was trying to gain access to my research. I thought it was . . . something else. But first that prowler, and now this . . ."

She was upset, and it made it hard for him to focus. "Do you remember anything else from that night?"

"No." For some reason, that seemed to infuriate her even more. "I should have paid more attention, but I . . . *He hit my car.*"

Derek went rigid. "He did *what?*"

"Slammed his fist right into the hood. I forgot to tell you that."

That changed everything. Someone trying to dig up information would have made himself scarce, not acted out like that. Derek didn't like this at all. The aggression wasn't a normal sign of espionage; it was much too personal.

She rubbed a hand across her forehead. "I want this to stop, Derek. I want this person caught."

"Breathe, Curie." He moved toward her, his fingers itching to touch her. Frenetic energy practically swirled around her. "Getting this worked up isn't going to help anything."

"Maybe not, but *this is something I can fight.*"

Her gaze caught his, and he saw her determination. This wasn't just about an intruder; she was talking about her sleep issues. She didn't like feeling helpless or vulnerable and, after reading about what she'd survived, he understood why. A girl from the wrong side of the tracks didn't make it big without having some scrappiness inside her.

"We'll fight it together," he promised. *"All of it."*

Unable to stay away from her a second longer, he kissed her. He started with soft, slow brushes to try to soothe her, but when he felt her kiss him back, all bets were off. Sealing their mouths together more intimately, he sent his tongue deep. Catching the small of her back, he pulled her against him. "You're so wired, you're ready to spark."

"I can't help it; I'm angry."

"Let me help you work off that head of steam." Her blue suit had some sort of wraparound jacket that tied at the side. He was more interested in the deep vee between her breasts. Using his chin, he opened it wider and pressed an openmouthed kiss against the center of her breastbone.

Her response was exactly what he'd hoped for. With a soundless cry, she arched back over his arm. Deliberately, he flattened his tongue against the sensitive spot and licked.

"Ohhh!" she cried, her muscles going taut. Her body vibrated like a violin string as he kissed and licked the erogenous zone.

When he felt her knees go, Derek picked her up. It had been a long, lonely night; he wanted all that frantic energy turned loose on him. He carried her to the couch, but the moment her weight settled onto the soft leather, she sprang up and scrambled away.

Breathing hard, she stared at him. "We can't."

"I think we've proven that we can."

"What about Ellen?"

"She won't bother us."

"She did in my dream!"

That stopped him. "You dreamed about us *here?*"

Shea blushed a thousand shades of red, which just about did him in. He'd known she'd dreamed about them together, but here? Where they'd had all those oh-so-nice platonic meetings? Moving fast, he went to the door. There was only so much a man could take.

Her eyes widened when he set the lock.

"Where?" he asked. "How?"

Her gaze flicked helplessly to the sofa, but she took another step back. Her heel banged against her brief-case, and she looked down at it, her expression turning guilty. They were two of a kind, he realized, wrapped up in straitjackets of responsibility. They were always expected to be conscientious, to do the right thing, to stay on the straight and narrow.

Well, he was tired of playing by the rules. He wanted to experience the thrills and risks that others seemed to take without compunction.

And he wanted to do it with her.

Catching her hand, he started to back up to the sofa. "Nobody has to know but us."

"But Derek—"

"It's your dream, Curie. Let me make it real."

Her eyes flared. All that energy was pulsing inside her, and he saw the exact moment it broke free.

"Take it off." Her hands shook as she reached for his tie. "Take it *all* off."

What the lady wanted, the lady got. Derek shrugged his jacket off his shoulders, and it hit the floor. He went for his shoes next.

When he righted himself, she nearly ripped off his shirt. He had to back away when her eager grip landed on his zipper. "I'll do it," he said, his teeth clenched. "Let me see you."

Her blue eyes went smoky, and the tie on her suit jacket gave way with one urgent pull. Derek swallowed hard as she stripped it off her shoulders. Like a heat-seeking missile, his gaze locked on her breasts. They bounced in the confines of her lacy bra, nearly spilling out of it. He peeled his tight briefs over his straining cock, but sat down hard when her skirt slid to her feet.

Everything on her matched. From her suit to her thong to her sexy high-heeled shoes, everything was a vivid royal blue.

But, oh God, those shoes.

With the suit, they'd been an intriguing spark. With the bra and thong, they looked downright racy. Striped like a zebra, they were sexy as hell.

He spread his arms across the back of the couch to keep from grabbing her. His cock wasn't as discreet. It pointed straight up at her, practically begging for her to come to him.

He watched as she undid the clasp of her bra and let it slide down her arms.

"You should star in your own commercials," he said, his voice like sandpaper. "You're sexier than any of those professional models."

She smiled at him and lifted her foot behind her to take off her sexy shoe. The position couldn't have been any hotter as she arched back to grab the heel.

"Leave them on," he ordered brusquely.

She paused as if momentarily uncertain, but when she looked into his eyes, her foot slowly lowered to the floor.

Soundlessly, she moved toward him. His fingers dipped into the back of the sofa, his nails rasping across the leather.

Oh, hell.

He *had* to touch.

He caught her by the hips as she came to a stop in front of him. Leaning forward, he pressed his lips to her hipbone. Her belly trembled, and he did the same to the other side. Wanting to get even more personal, he hooked his thumbs in the sides of her thong.

"Leave it on," she said when he started to pull the skimpy thing off of her. Her hand brushed through his hair. "I want you to take it off me later."

"Fuck," Derek breathed. He leaned his forehead against her stomach. That was the most erotic thing he'd ever heard. Every muscle in his body clenched, and he closed his eyes as he pulled on the reins.

Slow breaths. Inhale. Exhale.

"Sit back." Her voice was softer than a whisper.

He pulled back slowly, his gaze sliding up her gorgeous body.

She started toward him, then paused. Turning, she glanced over her shoulder as she lowered herself onto his lap.

Wrapping an arm about her waist, he pulled her close so that their bodies spooned together, his bigger form absorbing hers.

He groaned. "Good dream."

He nuzzled his face into the crook of her neck. He'd never felt anything softer or sleeker. She was all woman, and he couldn't get enough. Cupping her breasts in his hands, he felt her arch against him.

"Is this what you've been wearing underneath all those suits of yours?"

"Mmm hmm." She undulated against him, rubbing her butt against his raging cock. Back there, her thong was just one little strap. All he could feel was the stroke of her incredible skin. If she wiggled against him like that again, she might get a surprise.

She glanced over her shoulder, her big blue eyes full of heated arousal. "You asked that in my dream, too."

"What else would a red-blooded man ask?"

He palmed her breasts, lifting them higher. The pink tips jutted out and he rolled them between his thumbs and forefingers, making them redder and stiffer.

She groaned, and his right hand slid down her rib cage and belly to her panties, catching the damp crotch of her thong in his fingertips. The material strained under his pull, exposing the blond curls at the apex of her legs. "Now?"

She shook her head as her body rose and fell.

He groaned, the sound coming straight up from his diaphragm. She was trying to kill him.

He pulled his hand back up, stroked her belly again, but then sent it back down. They both watched as his fingertips slid under the blue lace.

"Derek," she groaned.

Using his knees, he spread her legs wider. He buried two fingers as deep inside her hot pussy as he could get and pressed his lips against her ear. "Want to know my fantasy? It involves bending you over that desk."

Her body squirmed, and she moaned so loudly that, for a minute, he did worry about his secretary checking on them. Then one of her arms came up and circled around his neck. Anything and everything outside his office disappeared.

"Deeper," she begged, lifting her hips higher.

He let his fingers plunge, and she let out a sharp cry. He drew out the sound by plucking at her nipple over and over again.

Her body strained and heaved, and with every brush of her soft bottom, Derek's cock jumped. It was so stiff and his balls were drawn up so tight, he ached.

"*Now*," he said, going for her thong again.

"Yes," she agreed, reaching down to help. She kept her other hand wrapped around the nape of his neck.

In a flash, he latched onto the flimsy piece of nothing with both hands. "Lift."

Her chest rose and fell as he slowly peeled the stretchy silk off of her. As soon as her pussy was bared he left the rest of the job to her, and resumed playing with her slick pussy and fondling her breasts. She twisted as she fought to get the panties off, and her spiked heels gouged into the carpeting.

Breathing heavily, she finally found her footing. When she glanced over her shoulder again, her eyes were wild with lust and need. There was no shyness this time when she looked down and found his cock. He felt her thigh muscles clench. Then she was lifting, positioning herself over him, and slowly dropping.

"Oh, God," she moaned as she slowly took in his throbbing erection.

Derek held her tighter as her head rolled back against his shoulder. He'd never felt anything so hot, so wet. She was tight, gripping him like a velvet fist. Inch by inch, she ate him up until she was seated right in the cradle of his lap. Her heat licked at him, and he deliberately ground himself up into her.

"Oh. *Oh!*"

Their bodies worked in pleasure as he pushed deeper and she flexed around him. Her thigh muscles tightened again, and then she caught the arm of the sofa for leverage as she began pistoning up and down. Her sexy high heels dug into the plush carpeting as they took her weight. Over and over again, she thrust herself onto him. Bumping, grinding, squeezing and releasing . . .

Derek was nearly lost. He wrapped himself around Shea, hugging her from behind. He stroked her straining body and murmured hot words into her ear.

Harder and faster, she worked herself on him. Her breasts juddered in his hands and her thighs quivered from exertion. He could feel the storm building and gathering within her. He began to thrust against her, his hips moving upward when hers came down.

"Derek!" she suddenly cried out.

Her back arched, and he buried his cock deep as her

pussy spasmed around him. He felt spurts of his own pre-come escape, and his head spun.

When she sagged against him, the mating instinct grabbed him by the throat. Turning her with him, he laid her facedown on the sofa. His hips began pumping hard, in sharp deep thrusts that he couldn't control.

Shea moaned and one leg bent reflexively so the heel of her zebra shoe was pointed upward in the air. He braced a hand beside her head, and she latched onto his wrist as he thrust into her repeatedly.

When his orgasm came, it kicked him in the back of the head and flat on the ass. He arched into her and lost all sense of time and space.

All he knew was her—his Shea.

When the world finally returned, his chest was pressed against her back, and her bottom cradled his hips. His deep, harsh breaths were puffing right beside her ear.

"Mmmmm," she murmured. A small wiggle rubbed her bottom against him.

Easing his weight from her, he wrapped his arms around her. When her fingers twined with his, Derek knew he was caught. Hook, line, and sinker. "We'll get the bad guys, Curie, I promise."

"All of them?" she asked softly.

"Every last one."

Ten

The creature was furious. A growl left his lips as he lay unmoving inside his beloved.

Why wouldn't she be with him anymore? The fog in her head was thicker, the weight of her body heavier. It had been nights and nights since she'd responded to his commands. He'd thought he'd found the answer to making her pliable, *functional*, but he couldn't keep working so hard. It used too much of his already dwindling power. He could feel his need growing, the tension and the friction. It was getting harder and harder to keep himself together. He needed her power or without it he was going to pull apart and become nothing.

"Wreakers," he hissed. "Wreakers numbering two."

This was their fault! They'd put a double whammy on her; it was the only answer. The Wreaker with the mean eyes had been hanging around, glomming onto her. It was getting harder and harder for the Somnambulist to find a way in, to find time to be with his one and only.

But the mean Wreaker wasn't here now. . . .

"*My* She-a. *Mine.*" Closing his eyes, the creature concentrated on her body—her wonderful, luscious, power source of a body.

It had to be her. Last night he'd gotten so desperate, he'd tried walking with the little boy next door. He'd needed the juice, but the little squirt had only given him a squirt. And when they'd pulled that kitten's tail, the boy had woken up! One delicious slash of claws across his wrist, and the crybaby had started sobbing.

The pain had only carried the Somnambulist so far.

He focused on his precious girl's achy spots. Those sensitive pink tips on her chest; that was where the answer lie. That, and the beguiling spot between her legs.

He summoned what power he had and sent it downward, concentrating on making her feel. The pink nubs tightened.

Yes, yes! That was what he needed.

He kept going, his power waning, until he finally gained control of an arm. He bent it, and her hand fell limply against the slick gown she wore. Using her fingertips, he rubbed one of the tickly buds through the material. Back and forth he flicked it, circling round harder and faster, pinching . . .

A moan left her throat, and relief swamped him. It was working. He moved her other hand to her chest and played with both the naughty nubs until they felt like they were on fire. Burning, aching, pulsing . . .

"Fire," he crooned. Visions of orange and yellow danced in his head.

He wanted to heat her up even more. The power she was giving him was invigorating, but it wasn't enough. He pushed her hands down, loving the waterlike feel of what she was wearing. When he got to the spot he so dearly wanted to investigate, one blunt brush of fingertips left him gasping. Oooh, he needed to get at that!

Rolling and contorting, he yanked the clothes off of her. At last she was bare, and all that wonderful skin was free to touch. Eagerly, he cupped her hands over the bumps on her chest and squeezed.

That magic spot down below squeezed, too, feeling all hot and tingly.

He threw one of her hands toward it.

"Ayiiii!" he yelped. What he found! She was soft and squishy down there: plump, hot, and wet. Her hips danced as he poked and prodded with her fingers. She bowed up like a bridge when he accidentally pushed a finger into a recess he hadn't expected; it felt so good!

He stuffed in another finger and drank up all the sensations he could. Heat, dampness, slickness, pressure, pleasure . . . He could feel what she was feeling inside and out.

Even better, she was moving without him! Her hips were rocking, and her legs were spreading. She was doing things he hadn't told her to do. He'd never heard of such a thing. Tilting her head up, he watched.

The picture was so exciting, he could barely stand it.

Yanking her other hand away from the pointy pink tip, he sent it down between her legs, too. She groaned, and the sound went right through him. She bent one knee, digging her heel into the mattress, and he touched and stroked and pushed her fingers into whatever openings he could find.

He gasped when he found a knot that sent spasms all through her. Greedily, he latched on, squeezing it tight as he kept her other fingers dancing.

"Oh," he moaned. The sound came out in her voice. The energy rolling through them was unlike any he'd ever felt as her hips bucked and swayed.

Then, suddenly, she went dead still.

"She-a?" The Somnambulist felt her muscles clench without his order. Panic exploded inside his chest. He couldn't get trapped. He couldn't— "She-*ahhhh!*"

The power exploded around him, almost more than he could bear. His head spun, and it took everything he had to keep from being kicked out of her. He held on to her tightly, lovingly, and gobbled it up until it was no more.

At last, her body collapsed on the bed and the power bled.

Right into him.

"Ahhhh," She-a sighed.

The creature's particles buzzed. She felt wonderful, rejuvenated. The cobwebs were gone, and the heaviness had evaporated. He felt wonderful, too.

Unstoppable.

Opening his hostess's eyes, he stared at the ceiling. Her vision had never been clearer. And her body was ready to go.

With a surge, he sat upright, taking her with him. As

powerful as he felt, he almost didn't need her body—but he wasn't leaving it behind. No way, no how. He whipped her legs off the bed, planted her feet on the floor, and stood. She didn't sway or falter.

She wasn't fighting him anymore.

He crowed in victory. "Oh, what fun we'll have tonight."

He directed her out into the hallway, but stopped quickly when he heard something.

He twitched her head and cocked it to the side. Another sound drifted up from the first floor, and his happiness drained away fast. Anger bubbled up to take its place. Why, why, why? Why must others interfere when he and his lovely were together? The Wreakers and the face in the window were always watching and intruding.

He started growling low. He'd had enough of this; she was *his*.

Turning, he stomped back into the room and looked around. The talking device on the little table by her bed caught his attention. He snatched it up and stared at the numbers. His beloved knew the right ones. Using her finger, he punched them in. A voice answered.

"Help me," the creature said. He liked the sound of his She-a's voice, so smooth and pretty.

He hung up and headed again toward the door.

He wondered how it sounded when she screamed.

The breeze was the first thing Shea noticed. It was soft, cool, and slightly damp. It blew against her face and ruffled her hair. She felt the soft strands tickle her bare shoulders, and her nipples contracted against the cool exposure. They were so sensitive, even that small stimulation put her body on high alert. Her thighs clenched, and she felt the dampness at their apex.

The sensation was pleasant and arousing, yet disconcerting.

Derek had left. Hadn't he?

Slowly, she became more aware of her surroundings. It was brighter than usual in her bedroom, even with her night-light. And something prickly poked against her feet, something damp and gritty.

Needles suddenly pricked at the back of her neck. She knew that feeling. She'd woken up feeling it once before.

She was outdoors.

That horrible awareness swept over her, the awareness that always came just as she was coming back into herself. Feeling vulnerable, she wrapped her arms around her middle . . . and realized she wasn't wearing any clothes. Her breath caught in her throat, and she curled into herself.

Feeling unbearably vulnerable, she waited that interminable time for her senses to fully return to her. When they did, her body braced.

She was near the parking lot, just at the edge of illumination of one of the streetlights. A car nearby suddenly roared to life, and her heart nearly burst out of her chest. Hurriedly, she jumped back into the shadows.

A whimper escaped her as it peeled out of the parking lot. She'd never felt so exposed in her life. She had to get inside!

She started backing quickly toward her home. She hadn't taken two steps, though, when her heel hit something big and solid.

"Ah!" she cried out as she lost her balance. Stumbling to her side, she nearly went down. Frightened, she spun around. She wasn't prepared for what she found. There, on her front lawn, was a body.

Her air seized in her throat, and her brain scrambled to process what she was seeing. A body. Facedown. Unmoving. A man.

Uncertain what to do, she edged around it. What had happened? Was he alive? Dead? *Had she had anything to do with this?* The band of tension around her ribs couldn't keep this panic at bay. When she saw the man's face, though, her horror spilled out into the darkness.

"Oh, no! No, no!" She dropped to her knees. "Phillip!"

She reached for him, barely able to think. He felt warm. Hesitantly, she ran her touch over him, searching for injuries. A cry left her lips when she found a knot on the back of his head. There was no blood, but the swelling felt as big as a tennis ball.

"Phillip?" she said shakily.

She shuddered when she saw a thick chunk of landscape edging at his side. "Oh, God."

Leaning over him, she checked for breath. Tears pricked her eyes when his soft air caressed her face.

Hand shaking, she felt for his pulse. It was strong and steady under her fingertips.

Yet he wasn't moving, and he wasn't waking up.

"Help me," Shea yelled.

Nobody answered.

"Help me!" she screamed.

And screamed and screamed and screamed.

Lights came on at the condo next door. The curtains shifted and then the door opened. Her neighbor Kathy peered outside. "Oh, my God! Shea? What's wrong?"

"He's hurt. Call an ambulance!"

Spinning around, her neighbor opened her closet door and pulled out a raincoat. "Steven," she called. "Dial 911!"

Shea rubbed her temple and tried to concentrate as the policeman asked her questions. It was impossible. The hospital corridor was blinding in its whiteness. The place was so cold and stoic, it was almost as if it was purposely reflecting all her emotions back onto her. With every second that passed, her doubts and worries grew.

"So what time did you find Mr. Morrison?" the man asked.

"Around midnight." That much she knew for sure.

"What was he doing there so late?"

Good question. "He's my friend."

"I see," the cop said. "Was he coming or going?"

"Coming." And she had no idea why.

"Have there been any other incidences in your neighborhood? Any break-ins or muggings?"

"No, nothing." Besides, it hadn't looked like a robbery to her. The EMT—Jason, she thought his name was—had found Phillip's wallet with his money and credit cards intact. It wasn't a good sign.

The cop scratched his ear with his pen. "Does Mr. Morrison have any enemies? Has anyone been harassing him or causing problems?"

Shea raked a trembling hand through her hair. She couldn't take this. She wanted to be in the emergency room with her partner. She wanted to apologize. She wanted to know if she was responsible!

"Dr. Caldwell? His enemies?"

She took a tight breath. "Not that I know of. Phillip gets along with nearly everybody."

"What about your business, this Biodermatics?"

"What about it?"

"Do you think the attack could have anything to do with that? Does anyone take issue with your products?"

She started to shake her head—until she thought of someone who'd tried to put his fist through the hood of her car. Her skin cooled. "We did have a trespasser recently."

"Did you report it?"

"Yes."

Her whirling brain honed in on the possibility. Could someone else have done this? It was a stretch, a long one, but it gave her . . . hope? God, how could she think like that? Phillip was lying unconscious in the emergency room. He'd been *attacked*.

And *she* was the one who'd been standing over his body.

She started to shake, out of control. She needed to tell the policeman everything. She had to tell him she might be responsible. She just couldn't get the words out of her mouth; she could barely fit them into her brain.

"I'm sorry, ma'am. I know this is tough. I have just a few more questions, if that's all right."

Shea stared at his badge so hard, it seemed to pulse. She'd been wandering around naked outside while Phillip had been hurt on the ground. What had that Somnambulist been doing with her tonight?

A sick, uneasy feeling corroded the lining of her stomach. She'd known it wouldn't like the more powerful sleeping pills she'd gotten from her doctor. Was this her punishment?

"Did you see anyone?" the cop asked. "Did you hear anything?"

Shea shook her head miserably. "When I found Phillip, I panicked. I wasn't paying attention to anything else."

That was the absolute truth. Trailing her fingers upward, she massaged the knot that had formed underneath her breastbone.

"I'll need to speak with Mr. Morrison as soon as he's able."

She nodded tightly.

She needed to speak to him, too. She had to know if she was to blame.

Footsteps suddenly sounded from the hallway, and a short sob escaped her when she saw Derek. He must have flown to get here so fast.

"Hey." He wrapped his arms around her and pulled her up tight. "Are you all right?"

She sagged against him, just sagged. "Better now," she whispered into his chest.

His embrace tightened, and she closed her eyes. She just needed to soak up his strength for a moment. Her fingers clenched into his back, and she realized he was out of his normal uniform of a suit and tie. For some reason, she found his jeans and black T-shirt even more comforting.

"What's going on?" he asked the policeman.

"I'm just asking Ms. Caldwell some questions, Mr. . . ."

"Oneiros. Derek Oneiros. I think she's had enough, Officer—" He peered more closely at the man's badge. "Dunn. Can you finish some other time?"

The cop scratched his ear with his pen again as he looked at his notes. "I'd like to get answers while everything's fresh in her mind, but yeah. I'll contact you if I think of anything else."

"Thank you," Shea said.

"Let's go sit in the waiting room," Derek said.

She went along numbly. She'd been on her feet ever since they'd rolled Phillip past those swinging doors at the end of the hall. How long ago had that been? Minutes? Hours?

The room was empty. Shea settled uneasily onto one of the couches and noticed vaguely that hospital waiting rooms had improved over the years. A television hung on the wall, and the magazines looked almost current. It hadn't been like this all those years ago when she'd waited to see her dad.

Another sob left her lips, and she dropped her head into her hands.

"Hey, easy now." Derek sat beside her, almost as tense as she was. Watching her closely, he rubbed her back. "How bad off is Phillip?"

It took her a while to find her voice. "He has a concussion. They'll have to run more tests to determine if it's worse than that."

Derek's gentle caress didn't stop. "He's young and strong. He'll be all right."

Lurching to her feet, she began to wander about the room. She needed to think. She needed to figure out what to do next. She had a problem. What was the next logical step?

"I'm sorry, I should have been there," Derek said.

"Don't say that!"

"I could have done something. I might have been able to stop it."

She shook her head hard. "No. It's best that you weren't there."

"The hell it is."

"It could have been you!"

Stark silence followed her words.

"Shea, what happened?" Derek finally asked. "What was Phillip doing there?"

"I don't know," she whispered. "I swear."

Their gazes connected, and she swallowed hard. Derek's hair was rumpled, but his eyes were sharp and intense. She'd gotten him out of bed—his bed—but he was here for her.

He wanted to help her, she knew that. She just couldn't—

Why not?

Her breath hitched. Why couldn't she tell him the truth? Was Phillip right? Was she too proud? Too ashamed?

The next logical step was sitting right in front of her. She didn't have to do this alone. She just had to do what Derek wanted: *trust him.*

"I have a new job for you," she said, gathering her courage.

"Anything. What do you need?"

"I want you to investigate someone."

His dark eyes narrowed, and he rose. "You think you know who did this."

"I need you to investigate *me.*"

He stopped. "You?"

Trust him.

"I need to know what I do at night," she said huskily. "I need surveillance or something, but not in person. Film me. I know you're not a private investigator, but the sleep clinic is booked solid. I can't get in, and—"

"Shea!" He caught her by the shoulders and gave her a little shake. "What are you trying to tell me?"

She took a shaky breath. "I have . . . I mean . . . I *am* a somnambulist. I walk in my sleep, Derek."

He sagged as if someone had just kicked the back of his knees.

"And I'm afraid I . . ." She swallowed hard. "I think I might have hurt Phillip."

Eleven

Derek was wound up tight when he pulled into the parking lot at Shea's complex. A Somnambulist. A fucking Somnambulist had entered her body and taken her over. He was so pissed, he was shaking. He knew what those things could do. He'd seen the havoc they caused. And to think of that leech toying with her—

Throwing the transmission into park, he ripped the key out of the ignition. When his hand slipped off the door handle, he realized he had to calm down and regain control. If he was going to track this thing down, he needed to think. It had circumvented him more than once. He needed to up his game, and he couldn't do that if he was seeing red.

Moving more precisely, he opened the door, then turned to face Shea's condo. Slowly, he exhaled through his mouth. He felt more contained—like a pressurized can ready to blow at the slightest prick—but it was the best he could do.

"Derek."

Glancing to his left, he found Cael. And Zane. For a moment he was surprised, but the more eyes and senses, the better.

"Man, I'm sorry about this." Cael shook his head. "A Somnie . . . *fuck*."

Yeah. Derek's fingers slowly curled into his palms. "Thanks for coming."

"Where's Shea?" Zane asked. "Is she okay?"

"She's at my place." He'd hated having to leave her. "She's trying to rest; she's just got too many questions."

"And she can't stop searching for answers?"

Derek looked at Cael in surprise.

His brother's eyebrows lifted sardonically. "Let's just say I know the type."

Okay, so he couldn't get his mind to turn off, either. Right now, Derek was relying on that as his greatest strength.

Zane came up beside him, looking concerned. "Is she alone?"

"Tony's with her. She's scared to even close her eyes now, but she took one look at him and figured he could reel her in if the worst happened."

"It won't." Cael's voice was calm. "Mack will watch over her from the dream realm."

Like a pit bull. Derek let out a long breath. That was the only reason he could let himself be here: he trusted that his brothers wouldn't let anything happen to her.

"So what are we looking for?" Zane asked.

Derek was *so* ready to get to work and do something proactive. He'd been strategizing during the entire drive over here. "She found Phil over there by the streetlight. I'm wondering if we can pick up any remnants of the Somnambulist. Sometimes when they're weak they'll leave a trail behind, particles of their essence."

"This one doesn't sound weak." Cael was already fanning outward to cover more area. "Still, there was an altercation. Maybe we'll get lucky and some of it detached."

"Stretch out with your senses," Derek told Zane quietly. He wasn't being condescending. Full-grown Somnambulists were rare—rare enough that even he hadn't caught on to what they were dealing with.

Without a word, they all started moving. Derek looked around vigilantly, trying to pick up every detail. The condo association kept its grounds well tended. The grass was trimmed, and the flowers were weeded. Everything seemed calm and peaceful, with "seemed" being the key word. Knowing what had happened here last night, the early morning sunshine felt out of place. Too bright. Too happy.

"I see you got rid of the noose."

Derek looked at Zane sharply.

His brother held up his hands. "I'm just saying it's been a while since I've seen you out of a suit and tie. I didn't think you owned jeans anymore."

"Zane," Cael said tiredly.

"What? He's loosening up. It's a good thing."

Loose? Zane thought he was loose? That was enough

to almost make Derek laugh. Almost. "Can we get on with this?"

"Yeah. Sorry, man. I'm just upset this thing got by me, all right?" Zane reached up to rub his shoulder. "I should have picked up on it."

"It's not your fault."

It was that sneaky nocturnal hitchhiker.

Derek started toward the streetlight. He hated to think of Shea waking up, not knowing where she was. How many times had that happened to her? It must be unnerving not to have that self-awareness that everyone depended on; to go to bed at night not knowing where you'd end up.

And that snake of a creature had taken her out of her home *naked*.

"Easy," Cael muttered underneath his breath.

Right. Easy. Control. *The Machine*.

It just wasn't working for him anymore.

As much as Derek tried, there was no way he could ignore the anger he felt or the sense of failure. The best he could do was compartmentalize it and use the energy to concentrate on what needed to be done.

Zane curled his fingers around the lamppost, but shook his head when he felt nothing. "Did you ever find out what Morrison was doing here?"

"The creature called him," Derek said.

"The Somnie? Are you freaking serious?"

"Freaking."

That was a good way to describe Shea's reaction, too.

When she'd finally gotten to see Phillip and he'd told her that she'd called, she'd nearly lost it.

"Did her partner see her sleepwalking?" Cael asked quietly.

"No, he was hit from behind." Derek shut down that picture decisively. "I'm getting nothing here. Let's go inside."

They headed back across the lawn and up the front walk. A few early morning risers looked at them strangely as the neighbors came outside to pick up their morning editions of the *Sentinel*. In this neighborhood, ambulances during the middle of the night drew attention. When they recognized Derek, though, Shea's neighbors went back inside.

Derek reached into his pocket as he came to the door.

"A key," Zane said, missing nothing. "Is that hers or *yours*?"

Derek's teeth ground together. He was not in the mood for this today. "Don't make me hit you."

"Sure it wouldn't make you feel better?"

He glanced at his brother sideways. It probably would, and Zane knew it. He had a cocky grin on his face and a "dare you" look in his eyes. The tension in Derek's shoulders drained. With a sigh, he reached out and tapped his brother on the head. "You're a pain in the ass."

"That's what they tell me."

Still, it worked for him.

The distraction worked, too. When Derek slid the key

into the lock he felt more settled, more centered. The door swung open, and he stepped inside with purpose.

Zane followed, but stopped not two feet inside the condo. "I feel it."

Cael bumped him aside and entered, too. "That's not the Somnambulist. That's leftover power."

The place was practically throbbing with it.

Derek's fingers buzzed as he went into the living room.

"How did I miss this thing?" Zane wondered.

"They're slippery," Cael said. "They catch sleepers before they call for us, right at the time they're most susceptible. Somnambulists slip in, take over, and draw the power they need."

He closed the door behind him. Moving about, Cael held his hands out, palms down, searching for any remnants of the creature. Trace elements might lead them back to it, but the odds were low after so much time had passed. Out of all the Oneiros brothers, though, he was one of the most powerful.

Derek followed suit. "This thing has to be old since it has the power to take over an adult. He's learned a lot of tricks to avoid us."

"It was there, wasn't it?" Zane said. "That night you took over with her?"

"Yeah," Derek admitted. "That humming vibration is their signature. It lowers as they mature, but I've never heard a bass like that. I should have figured it out."

Zane shook his head. "Let it go, man. Let it go."

He couldn't. Frustrated, Derek entwined his fingers

behind his neck. He hadn't been gone from Shea's bed for an hour when the thing had overtaken her. It had moved in when his back had been turned. He'd been administering to other charges when she'd needed him.

Cael took one look at his face and took the lead.

"Let's split up," he said. "Zane, look around down here. You know this place as well as Derek does. If you see anything out of place, let us know. Derek, why don't you head up to the bedroom? I'll go out to the car and get the cameras."

The door closed with a click as his older brother left, but instead of doing as he'd been instructed, Derek wandered farther into the living room.

"You don't want to think of it in there with her, do you?" Zane said quietly.

No, he didn't.

"I don't get it," Zane said. "I thought Somnies were playful, mischievous. Why would it hurt Phillip? He's Shea's friend."

"Somnies are playful when they're young." Derek glanced at the sofa where he and Shea had first made love and his fists clenched. "When they take over, though, they do it fully—there's no human consciousness there at all. The Somnambulist just taps into their host's abilities and knowledge. That's why when they're young, they'll do simple things like walk through the house, color, or stack up blocks. If we don't eradicate them early, they grow into more complicated activities. And they get more unstable."

Zane drummed his fingers against the kitchen counter. "Right. You look around here. *I'll* go upstairs."

Derek nodded. Good idea.

As soon as his brother left the room, he drew himself up. Shea was trusting him to help her, and he had no intention of letting her down. She just had no idea she'd put her faith in the one person—the one family—who could help her the most. He'd never been so grateful for his abilities and heritage.

Or so cursed for the knowledge he held.

This would be so much easier if he could just tell her what he was and that the "myth" was fact. He was a Dream Wreaker. She didn't have a sleep disorder; she had a parasite. He could get rid of it; destroy it with one touch of his hand, or scare it away forever. If she'd just sleep with him, she'd be safe. A Somnambulist would never come into a Wreaker's bed.

He just couldn't tell her any of that. He wouldn't even know where to start.

"Shit." He rested his elbow atop the fireplace mantel and rubbed his forehead.

It was then that he noticed the photographs she kept there, one in particular. It showed two smiling people wearing matching Mets caps at a game at Shea Stadium. One, though, had more of a half-smile. The left side of the man's face was disfigured, pulling his lip out at an odd angle. The arm he'd wrapped around Shea's shoulders showed scarring, too.

Burn scars.

Slowly, Derek picked up the photograph. The man was older than Shea, but his blond hair left no doubt as to whom he was. Neither did the love in his matching blue eyes.

"Ah, Curie," he said softly.

Her dad was the one who'd been hurt in that fire—the fire that had burned their trailer to the ground.

Gently, Derek put the photo back in its place of honor. No wonder she slept with a night-light on. No wonder the fireplace under the mantel was clean as a whistle. No wonder her nightmares always had flames.

"You all right?" Cael asked from the doorway.

Derek turned to see his brother juggling three cameras in his arms, and he quickly went over to help. "Thanks for these," he said. "They'll make her feel better, even though we don't need them."

"Thank Devon," Cael replied. "She begged and borrowed to get us three with motion detectors. For God's sake, don't drop that one; it's hers."

Derek nodded. Cael's girlfriend was fitting into their family just fine. Being a beautiful redhead, she had most of the Oneiroi panting after her, willing to be at her beck and call. Touch one of her cameras, though, and she could get strict fast.

Looking down, Derek fiddled with the camera strap. "Listen, man. I think I came down too hard on you when you were going through that stuff with Devon. I didn't know. I didn't understand—"

"It's all right."

"No, it's not. You didn't want to leave her. You *couldn't*. At the time, I didn't understand why you didn't just do your job and treat all your charges equally." He leveled his look on his big brother. "I get it now."

Cael's chest expanded as he took a slow, heavy breath. "Sounds serious."

"It is."

"Are those cameras for the bedroom?" Zane suddenly asked from the staircase. "Kinky!"

Cael rolled his eyes.

"You're the one who brought him with you," Derek said.

"Don't remind me."

As it turned out, though, it was a good thing both his brothers had come to help. Cael was a good photographer in his own right and knew what camera angles would catch the most of the rooms. Zane, unfortunately, knew Shea's night habits best. Being barred from her nighttime bed, Derek could only defer to his little brother on that one.

That was going to change, though, and soon.

"How's that?" Zane asked, moving a pillow on the living room sofa out of the line of sight.

"Good. Right there." Cael's head came up from the viewfinder, and he pressed a button on the camera.

The phone suddenly rang, startling all three of them. Quickly, Derek walked over to the end table and picked up the receiver. "Hello?"

There was a pause. "I'm sorry, I must have the wrong number."

"Hold on. Are you trying to reach Shea Caldwell?"

"Yes. Who is this?"

He checked the caller ID. It was the Biodermatics office. "This is Derek Oneiros."

"Oh, Mr. Oneiros. This is Lynette Fromm. Your security staff is over here right now."

The new secretary. Derek waved off his brothers.

"What's going on?" she asked, irritation clear in her voice. "Your people have activated ID-only access to most of the offices, and they've limited my computer account. I can't do anything."

"There was an incident last night involving Ms. Caldwell and Mr. Morrison. Neither will be at work today."

There was another long pause. "Are they in trouble?"

"Everything will be fine. Can you and Tamika handle things?"

Lynette let out a huff. "Well, I don't know what I can do with your people underfoot, and I have no idea where Tamika is."

Derek's head snapped up and his eyes met Zane's. "Tamika hasn't made it in to work yet?"

"No. What's going on? And why are you at Dr. Caldwell's house? I thought she and Phillip were together—"

"Lynette," he said sharply, "I know you haven't been there long, but do what you can. Shea will be in touch soon."

"She will? Oh, okay . . . I'll do my best."

"Good," Derek said firmly, hanging up.

"Tamika didn't call for REM sleep until late last night," Zane said.

"After the attack?"

"Yeah." Zane turned toward the door. "I'm going to go find out where she is and what she's been doing."

Just as he was about to grab the doorknob, it turned. He jumped back when the door opened and a big form appeared over him. "Tony! You scared the shit— Oh! Hi, Shea."

Derek pivoted swiftly. There, in the doorway, stood Shea and another of his brothers. Compared to muscle-bound Tony, she looked petite and vulnerable. The look was deceiving; she wasn't weak at all. Her eyes were as bright as anyone's in the room. The set of determination in her jaw, though, was matched only by one. His.

Derek covered the distance between them quickly. "What are you doing here? You were supposed to try to get some sleep."

"I couldn't," she said simply.

Her eyelids fluttered when he brushed a soft kiss against her cheek. Still, when he hooked an arm around her waist, she didn't lean on him. She didn't pull away, though, either.

When she saw so many strangers watching her, she smoothed the blue scrubs she'd been given at the hospital the night before. She could have worn a potato sack and had his brothers at her feet.

"I'm sorry, but we haven't met," she said politely.

"I'm Zane." The youngest Oneiros eagerly stuck out his hand. He looked enraptured, totally caught.

Shea shook his hand, then held it. Tilting her head, she looked at him more closely. "*Do* I know you? You seem familiar."

Derek was just as surprised as Zane was.

"I've been around the neighborhood," his brother said, covering quickly.

Shea nodded, not quite convinced. She seemed to still be trying to place him when she caught sight of the other man in the room. "You must be Cael. Thank you for coming. This can't be easy for you."

"You ask for the help of one Oneiros brother, you get us all."

Almost hesitantly, Shea looked around her home. "Did you find anything?"

"Not yet." Derek's fingers tightened against her waist, pulling her closer. She looked so tired, yet so determined and brave. "Nothing looks out of place to me. Maybe we just need to wait for Phillip to—"

"There's mud on the floor."

"What?" He followed her gaze across the room. He and his brothers had been searching so hard for supernatural evidence, he hadn't noticed anything so mundane. Yet there it was, dirt scuffed here and there . . . footsteps.

Human footsteps, not the trace of a night creature.

En masse, his brothers moved. Zane yanked open the sliding glass door. "It's unlocked."

"Check out the area," Derek said, taking charge.

They all stepped into the backyard, with Tony and Zane heading for the bushes that lined the edge of the property. Cael went farther out in the communal backyard of the six condo units.

"Here," Derek said. There were footprints in the

flowerbed under Shea's kitchen window—footprints with the toes facing the building.

"Those aren't mine," Shea declared decisively.

"You sure?" Tony asked.

The footprints looked like they'd been made by tennis shoes. Runner's shoes. Stretching out her foot, she placed it carefully next to the prints.

"I'm sure." Her foot didn't fill the track.

They all looked at each other.

"How old could those prints be?" Derek asked.

Zane scratched his temple. "Less than a day. We got that short burst of rain yesterday afternoon. Remember?"

Shea cleared her throat. "I walked in my sleep the other night. The next morning, I found my shoes lined up in front of the kitchen sink." She rubbed her arms. "They were pointed out here, as if I should look out the window."

Derek exchanged a stunned look with his fellow Dream Wreakers.

"Do you think it was trying to tell her somebody was out there?" Zane whispered.

"*It?*" Shea said, catching the slip.

"You and Phillip weren't the only people here last night," Derek said, changing the topic quickly. "These footprints are proof that you had a Peeping Tom."

"Or a Peeping Tammy," Tony countered. "Those are small feet for a man."

Shea's eyes rounded. "The car! Oh my God, how could I have forgotten?"

She whirled toward them. "I heard a car in the parking lot last night. It was trying to get out of there fast. I just . . . I just wasn't coherent then."

"Could you identify it?" Derek said. "Did you see the make or model? Did you get a look at the driver?"

Her face fell. "No."

First the trespasser at her place of business, and now this? "Baby, I don't want to scare you, but I think your problem's worse than an overaggressive business competitor. I think you've got a stalker," Derek said.

"A stalker!"

"You've caught someone going through your garbage, rummaging around your desk, and now watching through your windows. Maybe worse."

Her eyes went wide. "But why? And why would they hurt Phillip?"

"He's too close to you? Maybe he stumbled upon them? I don't know. These people don't have normal thought processes."

"But who would do something like this?"

"I don't know, but I'm not taking any more chances. I'm moving in," Derek said firmly.

Shea took an instinctive step back. "No."

"Yes," he said, walking toward her. He caught her hand before she could step away again. "Either that, or you move in with me. You're not going to be alone."

"I can't go to your place," she said tightly. "I don't know the layout."

Meaning she was sure she'd sleepwalk again.

"Then it's decided," he said. "I'll bring my things over today."

She looked up at him, her face drawn. It was obvious she didn't like the idea, but she knew she was in danger. "Fine, but you're sleeping in the guest bedroom."

Zane coughed loudly.

He gasped for air even louder when Tony elbowed him in the gut.

Shea wasn't finished. "You'll be in another bedroom with the door locked and the dresser pulled in front of it."

Cael turned away and became inordinately interested in the garden hose.

"Oh, come on, Curie," Derek said coaxingly.

"No. That's the way it has to be. I will *not* wake up to find you lying unconscious at my feet."

His brothers' heads turned with a snap.

"And I won't find you standing in the headlights of my car when I'm sleep driving." Shea ignored the gasps. She kept her blue gaze on his as she fisted her hands into his T-shirt. "I just *can't*."

Twelve

Derek found Shea in her bedroom. She was standing quietly, staring at the camera Cael had placed on her dresser. With the way the morning sunlight gleamed off her blond hair, she looked angelic, almost peaceful. Yet an aura of energy buzzed around her.

Leaning against the doorframe, he simply watched her. He wished he knew what to say to her . . . What to do . . . Hell, he knew exactly what he had to do. He had to rip that thing out of her and obliterate it.

But how could he make her feel better without telling her the full truth?

"You're looking at me again." Slowly, Shea turned. When her tired blue gaze met his, Derek felt the kick right in his gut.

"Can't be helped," he said gruffly. "You shouldn't still be up."

She shrugged. "Can't be helped."

She was clearly exhausted, mentally and physically. So was he. A night without sleep could do that to a normal person, and he was anything but normal.

Over the hours, the night had increasingly pulled at him. The darkness had called. His charges had called. Ignoring the relentless tug had him drained. Yet as much as the sunlight hurt his eyes and the rising temperature sapped his strength, he didn't care. He wasn't going to sleep until she did.

"Are your brothers gone?"

"Tony just left."

Cael and Zane had gone to check on Tamika a while ago—not that she needed to know that.

Shea nodded. "They're good guys. Handsome. If I didn't know better, I'd believe you *were* descended from Greek gods."

Derek's pulse jumped, but he let the subject pass. She was in no condition to deal with any more shocks.

"I'm having trouble thinking straight," she admitted quietly.

"How can I help?"

Agitated, she drummed her fingers against her elbow. "I need you to be straight with me. Is there really a chance I didn't hurt Phillip? Even the smallest chance? Because if not, I need to refocus and prepare. I can't do that now, because this feeling of hope is getting in the way—and I hate that it's hope."

"Believe it." She hadn't done this—he was one hundred percent certain. The Peeping Tom or the Somnambulist was responsible. He didn't care which, but it hadn't been her.

Unable to watch her like this any longer, he pushed

away from the doorframe. The tingles of energy he'd felt randomly coming off of her suddenly focused in his direction. The jolt was sexy, magnetic. It drew him right to her, and he stopped only when the toes of their shoes brushed.

"Somebody put those footprints on your carpet," he said, reasoning with her. He ached to touch her, but knew she needed to deal with this first. "You didn't hit Phillip."

Her chin came up. "That other person might have been coming to his rescue."

"Or *you* might have. You said your hands were empty when you came awake."

"But Phillip said I called him. Derek, I lured him over here."

"No, you called him for help." Besides, she hadn't called anyone; the Somnambulist had pulled that little stunt.

Worry slowly dimmed her eyes. "But did I really need it? It's . . . I'm becoming more aggressive when I sleepwalk. I already told you that."

That little sleep driving story still made Derek light-headed. He couldn't believe how far the creature had gone with her! *To put her behind the wheel of a car . . .* "Your stalker is becoming more aggressive, too. There were three people here last night, one of whom was not invited yet somehow got into your home."

Shea rubbed at her breastbone. "I can't believe I'm hoping you're right. I'm *hoping* I have a stalker. I'm *hoping* he or she attacked Phillip. It's wrong on so many levels."

Yet Derek needed her to accept the fact, unpalatable as it might be. The Somnambulist was one thing, but this unknown third party threw everything out of whack. He needed her to help him figure everything out, and the sooner she stopped blaming herself, the better.

She rubbed at her breastbone harder with the heel of her palm. "I feel like I should have known. The face in the window . . . Maybe I did know."

"The face in the window?"

She jumped. Sighing, he drew her back toward him and brushed his thumb against her cheek. "Sorry, it's just rare for Somnambulists to—"

She flinched again.

"Sleepwalkers," he quickly clarified. "It's rare for sleepwalkers to remember anything they see or do."

Even as he tried to calm her, though, Derek's own mind was spinning. It was more than rare; he'd never heard of anything like that happening before. A Somnambulist *never* transferred its consciousness to its host. Never.

An uneasy feeling settled in his chest. Was that thing so entwined with her? Were they meshing so completely?

Would hurting it hurt her?

And killing it . . . Oh, God.

"Derek?"

He kissed her. He just pulled her against him and sealed his mouth against hers. Put him up against a Night Terror any day. Make him face an army of Luna-

tics. He could take a threat against himself. Just don't
threaten her—he couldn't handle it.

His touch seemed to finally break her. With a soft cry,
her arms wrapped around his neck. Her body melted
against his, and something inside his chest squeezed.
He circled an arm around her waist and pulled her even
closer. He wanted to protect her from this. He wanted to
shield her from everything bad and scary.

Pulling back, he looked into her eyes. "I just wish
you'd let me stay."

Any remaining color drained from her face.

"Don't say that," she whispered hoarsely. Her fingers
clutched at his shoulders. "Don't say that."

Almost desperate, she pulled him back down. Her
kiss was deeper, more raw. Her tongue swept through
his mouth frantically and her hands tugged his T-shirt
from his jeans.

She needed this. They both needed this.

Derek's hands fisted into the loose-fitting scrubs.
Breaking their kiss, they tugged off clothing and dropped
it onto the floor, then came back into each other's
embrace. Derek groaned when Shea pressed her palm
against his stiff cock.

"I hate what's happening to me," she whispered
hoarsely against his chest. "I can't take not knowing
what I'm doing, and feeling so out of control."

He pumped into her hand. "Baby, you can be in
charge of this."

The feel of her soft palm and fingers was almost too
much. He'd needed to be with her like this ever since

she'd first called from the hospital. The fear and anguish in her voice had been too much. He'd do whatever she wanted, be whatever she needed.

Their gazes connected, and the temperature in the room rose by at least ten degrees. Heat was suddenly pouring through his veins. The tips of her breasts brushed against his chest, and his balls drew up tight. Her belly stroked against his aching cock, and it was all he could do not to thrust into her right then and there.

But she wanted to be in charge, and he'd given her the reins.

She gave him a soft nudge backward. The back of his knees hit the mattress, and he sat down hard. He let out a ragged breath when she stepped between his knees, naked and vulnerable.

She placed one knee on the mattress beside his hip, and he slid his hand intimately between her legs. With a slow groan, her head fell back. Her hair dangled behind her, and she looked so sexy he almost forgot to breathe. He rubbed her mound more possessively, and her breasts jutted up into the air.

"Come here, baby."

Her eyes were heavy-lidded as she climbed fully onto his lap, straddling him. Watching her closely, Derek cupped her ass. The sheets rasped beneath her knees as he pulled her forward. His lips pressed hard against hers, and he swept his tongue across her damp lips. They parted, and she sank down onto him.

It was the most sensuous feeling in the world. Derek's heart thundered as her hands glided up and down his back. Her breasts flattened against his chest, and her belly pressed tightly against his cock. His proprietary instincts surged, and he fisted a hand in her soft hair.

He hated the thought of anyone or anything else touching her. Permeating her.

Watching her.

"Ah, hell." He suddenly pulled her tighter against him and tried to shield her with his hands.

He glanced over her shoulder toward the dresser. "The camera," he said, breathing harshly. "It's motion activated. I was supposed to turn it off until tonight."

She slowly looked over her shoulder. Staring right at the camera lens, she took a deep breath. When she turned back to him, a look of determination was on her face. "It's always smart to run a test sample."

Oh. Fuck.

Shea felt Derek's cock jump against her belly—but she wasn't trying to be bold or outrageous. She needed this. She needed him. She needed him to make her feel like she was whole, not splintering into two. At night, she turned into a nameless, faceless personality. In the daylight, she was Shea.

Very aware of the prying eyes, she kissed him again, loving how big and tough he felt, so solid. Sensuously, she rubbed herself against his muscled chest. His shoulders flexed, as did his hands. She felt them settling onto her backside again—not shielding her from the camera, but cupping her, caressing and molding her.

She groaned and swiveled her hips against him. Rubbing her pussy against his thick cock, she shivered. "There was a time I thought I liked you for your brain."

He grunted. "Right now, I couldn't spell my name."

Lifting herself up higher, Shea directed her breast toward his mouth. A delectable tension streaked through her body when he latched onto her nipple and began to suckle intently. Rolling her head to the side, she watched as his mouth worked on her. She saw the indentations in his cheeks, felt the hot lashes of his tongue, and heard the wet sounds. She closed her eyes as she felt her pussy clench.

Then she was wet.

She moaned when the full head of Derek's erection brushed against her, and she started to lower herself onto him.

He restrained the movement, keeping her lifted and poised for his mouth. When he moved his hot, wet attention to her other nipple, she squirmed in his grip.

"I thought I was in control."

"Curie," he said, raking his teeth against her swollen tip, "in case you haven't noticed, you've got me wrapped around your little finger."

She let out a sharp cry when he began suckling again, pulling at her, tugging so hard, she felt hot flashes deep in her womb. Cradling him against her, she ran her hands up and down the straining muscles of his back.

She'd show him what a little finger could do.

Deliberately, she trailed it down his spine. His grip bit into her butt, and his mouth opened wider against her, taking more and more of her breast into the hot wet cave of his mouth. She bent over him, reaching farther and farther. The small of his back shivered, and his ass clenched. He went dead still when she slid her pinkie into the crack between his rock-hard cheeks.

"Christ," he said, suddenly fighting for air.

Pressing his face between her breasts, he began loving her there. He licked, kissed, and rubbed his stubble against the sensitive spot until she was creaming so hard, she was close to coming.

Cradling the back of his neck, she felt him breathing hard against her. His air was warm and moist. Encouraged, she pressed deeper. He bucked hard when the pad of her little finger stroked over his back door.

"Shea," he said, his voice ragged.

She stroked again and then let her finger lie against him, intimate and brash.

"Fuck. Me," he panted.

"I will," she said silkily into his ear.

Slowly, he lay back, trapping her hand underneath him—and keeping her finger clenched tightly into place.

Shea came up over him and braced her free hand against the mattress by his head. She felt his hands moving between her legs, positioning his cock against her. Closing her eyes, she slowly pressed herself down onto that wonderful thickness.

Yet, she stopped with a jerk mid-stroke.

Her eyes popped open, and their gazes locked. His eyes were heavy, seductive, and just a little wild.

He pressed his finger more firmly against the bud of her anus, watching her.

"Oh, God," Shea groaned. Her heart beat a tattoo against her rib cage. Frozen, she stared into his eyes as he stroked the back of her thigh with his other hand. He looked so dark and sexy. So *hers*.

That intimately placed finger stroked deeper between her legs. He rubbed her swollen pussy lips. Getting more intimate, he caressed her opening, massaging the muscles as they stretched wide around him. Her inner muscles fluttered, making him groan.

Gathering up her moisture, he brought his finger back to the bud of her anus. He slicked it deliberately, watching her. "You're in control," he said. "Do what you want."

Do what she wanted.

Oh, God.

She didn't think. She just began pressing herself downward onto his stiff, hot erection—and onto his penetrating middle finger.

Shea bit her lip as she took him both places. With every millimeter she sank onto him, the double pressure built. The fullness . . . It was . . . It felt . . . Oh, God.

Her heart began to pound uncontrollably, and her mind spun. Dipping her head, she licked her tongue deliberately across his nipple—and pressed more firmly against his own secret place.

"God, Shea!"

"Ah!" she cried out sharply when his hips bucked. His cock rammed into her, and friction raked against her sensitive clit.

Her back arched, and her fingers clenched his ass

tighter. Their bodies strained, caught in the position, too wracked with pleasure to give it up.

But then her finger slipped.

And his legs churned.

And the need to move slammed into her.

Leaning on her supporting arm, she began to pump. Up and down she went, accepting him deeply. She took his finger up her ass, and then two. The dark pleasure had her nipples stiffening to tiny, aching points. Cramped as it was, she moved her hand underneath him, feeling him and tickling him.

Sweat built up between their bodies. Shea felt a droplet trail along her back where the camera was focused, documenting exactly what he was doing to her and what she was doing to him.

Voyeuristic pleasure had her grinding down on him, taking his fingers to the hilt, and she began to come. She came so hard that her back arched, her elbow buckled, and her fingers clenched. That little finger of her right hand curled inward and found a home.

The tight, hot penetration had Derek groaning.

Then his hips were straining upward, lifting her right off the mattress. He rammed into her twice before he exploded. Pressing up into her, he held her immobile as his seed spurted for what felt like forever.

Dropping onto the bed as one, they both fought for air. Coherency took a long time coming.

Shea cuddled against Derek's chest, loving the safety she found there. His arms wrapped around her, keeping her close.

"Better?" he asked softly.

So much.

"Thank you," she whispered. "For coming to the hospital. For dealing with . . . everything."

"You should have told me about the sleepwalking before." His lips brushed against the top of her head. "How long has this been happening?"

She hesitated. "Since I was eleven or twelve."

His head pulled back sharply, and she glanced up at him.

"You've been walking in your sleep since you were twelve?"

"Oh, no. It stopped after . . . It stopped for a while." Absently, she ran her hand across his chest, tracing the lines of the muscles she found there. It was hard to talk about this. Growing up, she'd had to deal with the laughs and the teasing—or worse, the frightened looks. Yet she felt so close to him, like she could tell him anything.

Almost anything.

"It just started again recently," she said. "The night before I came to you for the background check on Lynette, actually."

He stared up at the ceiling. "That explains the fear."

"What?"

"Nothing," he said, rubbing her back. He swept his hand down to her bottom, holding her so their bodies wouldn't disconnect.

Even satiated, she liked the feeling of him inside her.

It made her feel secure and protected. Almost loved.

She felt fatigue falling over her like a blanket, and tried to push it off. It was just so difficult, wrapped in his arms. She could feel his intelligence and his masculine strength.

"You know," he said quietly, "the Oneiroi don't like it when things mess with their charges."

Shea went still. Derek Oneiros didn't seem like the type to tell bedtime stories. "Their charges?" she prompted, wanting more.

"Those people placed in their care, the ones to whom they deliver dreams. We fight to protect them."

She looked at him in bemusement. "I didn't think the Oneiroi took sides, good or evil."

"We don't."

She smiled. *We.* She knew he was coddling her, indulging her, but she liked it. It was sweet and so very soothing. Her eyelids felt heavy, and it was getting hard to concentrate.

The look in his eyes was steady. Intense. "We're very protective about our right to bestow dreams. Good or bad, we don't like it when something gets in our way."

"Like a Somnam— Like sleepwalking?"

His eyes sparked. "Precisely."

She felt something flare inside her chest. He looked so serious, and she'd always loved fairy tales. Good overcoming evil. The impossible coming true. "So what do you do about it?"

"We stop it."

That heat in her chest intensified, but it wasn't that constant fear she was always trying to tamp down. "And you're my Oneiros?"

"I am."

She inhaled slowly. She liked the sound of that. Her heart pounded as she cupped his cheek. "You'll protect me?"

"You know I will."

The promise touched her. But—

"From the other room, though. Right?"

She was nearly under, but she forced her eyelids back open so she could make sure he got her point.

He sighed. "From the other room."

"With the door locked." One last thought occurred to her, and she lifted her head sharply off his chest. "Don't let me fall asleep naked."

"Don't worry, Curie." He cupped the back of her head, and drew her down. "I've got you covered."

Thirteen

When Shea awoke, it was strangely dark. Not quite night, but not quite day . . . The eerie grayness threw her, and she was disoriented as to time and place. A long, low rumble made her turn on her side.

She was in her bedroom. Alone—she glanced down quickly—and dressed. She smoothed her hand over Derek's black T-shirt. It was soft and comfortable. Comforting. Outside, she heard another low rumble.

Thunder.

She looked out the window. The sky was heavy and foreboding; a summer storm was about to hit.

Reaching out, she turned on her bedside lamp. The cloud layer was so thick, it blocked out the sun. The resulting darkness was nearly as unnerving as the dead of the night, yet she was surprised when she saw her alarm clock. It was still early afternoon. She'd slept deeply, but had she slept soundly?

Sitting up, she looked cautiously about the room. Everything seemed in order.

She got up, Derek's T-shirt brushing low against her thighs as she headed toward the hallway. She found him asleep in her guest bedroom—with the door standing wide open.

Peeved, she pushed her hair over her shoulder. Yet as she watched him, it was impossible to stay upset with him. He lay sprawled on his back, taking up most of the queen-size bed. The bed linens were slung low across his hips. Very low.

He was gorgeous, his body muscled and tanned. His hair was rumpled, and his eyelashes looked long and soft against his cheeks. Her breasts ached when she saw the stubble darkening his features. Those prickly whiskers made him look rakish and reckless.

Knowing he was the exact opposite made this private little viewing even more intimate.

Wind suddenly blew strong against the walls of the condo, but Derek slept deeply, oblivious to the impending wildness outside. He'd been as tired as she was, maybe more. He hadn't had adrenaline pumping through his veins the way she had, but he'd stayed with her throughout the night. He'd held her hand, calmed her nerves, and fended off his own fatigue.

Lightning flashed. Giving in to an impulse, Shea crossed the room and carefully crawled onto the bed beside him. She hesitated as she watched him. He didn't turn toward her, he didn't adjust to the movement of the mattress, and he didn't grumble. Thunder cracked, making her jump. Still, Derek did nothing.

She'd been right; he slept like the dead.

He *was* vulnerable.

As big, smart, and strong as he was, he couldn't defend himself against something he didn't see coming. He was susceptible to dangers like her or anything else that wandered in the night.

She edged toward him. When he still didn't respond, she laid her head on his shoulder. Her arm found a comfortable spot around his waist, and her leg twined around his. For a long time, she lay there thinking.

It was time she made some decisions.

It could have been five minutes; it could have been half an hour. Still, when Derek suddenly stretched, it surprised her. His whole body shifted as if he'd just come back into himself. Shea watched in fascination. She knew how that felt, but she'd never seen anyone else do it before. A pleasant warmth filled her when his dark eyes opened.

"Mmm," he said, his arm instinctively coming around her. "Now *this* is the way to wake up."

"Good morning," she whispered.

"More like good afternoon." Pulling her close, he kissed her. The long, slow, drawn-out welcome stopped only when another blast of wind rattled the windows. Turning, he lay so they faced one another. "Did you sleep well?"

"I think so."

"Good dreams."

Her eyes narrowed. It didn't sound like a question, and she *had* had good dreams—insights about her research, actually. His bedtime story about the Oneiroi popped into her head, but she pushed it away. As tempting as it was to believe in make-believe, she had to face the truth.

"You didn't lock the door," she said accusingly.

He glanced toward the hallway. "It's easier to hear if it's open."

"You didn't hear me when I walked in just now."

"I knew you were here." Once again, that calm assurance was in his voice.

She just couldn't fight it, and she didn't want to. She laid her hand against his chest. The rhythmic thud of his heart was steadying. "I've been thinking," she said.

"About what?"

"The things I need to do. The actions that will fix this situation." She looked into his eyes. "I need to tell the police the whole truth."

His hand tightened against her back. "Shea."

"I have a medical condition," she said, staying firm. "I'm under a doctor's care. There have been court cases where sleepwalkers have been declared not guilty, because they weren't in control of their faculties at the time the crime was committed."

"But we don't even know if you did commit the crime."

"Which makes it even more important to get everything on the record." She ran her hand over his bicep. The strength she found there encouraged her. "If somebody has been stalking me, I want to do something about it."

He stared at her for a long moment. "All right. Whatever you need."

She found herself needing *him* more and more each day. That was why her next decision was so important.

"I've also made a decision about my sleepwalking."

One of his eyebrows lifted. "You have, have you?"

"I wasn't thinking clearly last night when I asked you to monitor me. It's not fair to you, and it's dangerous. I need to seek professional help." Her fingers curled against his smooth skin. "Since they can't get me into the sleep clinic here, I'm going to have Dr. Wainright refer me to somebody. I don't care if I have to fly halfway across the country. I want to see a specialist."

In one fluid motion, Derek propped himself up on his elbow. "Stay with me. Just give it a little more time."

"I need to do this."

"Sleeping pills are not the answer. You've already determined that."

"There might be something else wrong. I could have an electrical short in my brain, an out-of-time circadian rhythm, or ment—" She took a deep breath. "Mental—"

"There is nothing wrong with you."

She cupped his cheek, the tension in the room growing as surely as the storm outside. Feeling miserable, she looked at him. "Please don't fight me on this."

A muscle worked in his temple, and she could see the strain in his jaw.

"Fine," he said at last. "I'll come with you."

She didn't know why his offer surprised her, but it did.

"But your company," she argued. "You've been spending so much time away from there already."

"I have good people. They'll cover for me."

So did she.

Or did she?

Oh, God! With a jolt, she sat upright. She couldn't believe she'd left her company stranded high and dry. "I forgot to call in. I should have shut down for the day."

Derek drew her back down. Sliding one leg between hers, he kept her in place. "I had my people step in. We didn't interfere with production, but we locked down your office, Phillip's office, and your lab."

Shea exhaled roughly and looked to the ceiling. "Thank you. I . . . I wasn't thinking."

"You were thinking plenty; you just had other things on your mind." Derek's hand was gentle as he tucked her hair behind her ear. "Curie, we need to talk."

Her stomach dropped. She knew where he was heading, and she didn't want to have this conversation.

"Who do you think is behind all of this?" he asked.

She clutched at the sheet. "I don't know."

"When we talked at my office, you were worried that this might be an inside job."

"That was when I thought someone was trying to access company info, not kill my partner!"

He wound a strand of her hair around his finger. As calm as he looked, the electricity crackling in the room nearly overpowered that outside. "I want you to think back to that prowler. I know you were disoriented, but could it have been a woman?"

Oh, God. The footprints. "You think it was the same person outside my window."

"Just close your eyes and try to remember."

She didn't have to close her eyes. That part of the night was very clear in her memory. She remembered the dark shape and its anger. "The person was wearing a loose-fitting sweat suit with the hood pulled up. It . . . it could have been anybody."

"I'm just exploring all the angles," he said gently. "Someone—maybe a woman—has been watching you. They gained access to your office, and Phillip was attacked. I'm trying to find the common link."

Shea bit her lip. "But that narrows it down to Tamika or Lynette."

"If you have other thoughts, I'm open to them."

She swallowed hard.

He ran a finger gently along her temple. "It would be difficult for anybody else to gain access to your office without drawing attention. Have either of them been acting suspicious?"

"Both of them." Shea rolled onto her back. She couldn't bear to think it was someone that close to her.

"Tell me what you've noticed."

She hated this, absolutely hated it. "Tamika's personality has changed recently. She's always tired and cranky."

"Like she could be running around at night, looking into other people's property?"

Shea closed her eyes. "She's a good friend of mine . . . or so I thought."

"Good friend or not, she wasn't at work this morning."

Shea looked at him sharply. "Where was she?"

"We don't know, but coming right after the attack, it looks suspicious. Lynette was there alone."

"Oh, no."

"You don't trust her."

Shea plucked at Derek's T-shirt. "Let's just say I don't know her well enough yet. She seems to want to get into everything."

"All this started when she showed up."

"But that could be coincidence. You did the background check on her."

He shifted. "Yeah, and on the surface she checks out. She has no criminal history, her credit is solid, and her former employers liked her. But I'm still trying to get more information on her sabbatical during her stepmother's illness."

"I don't think she likes me," Shea admitted.

His eyebrows drew together. "Why do you say that?"

"She's passive-aggressive. I thought it might be just a defense mechanism, but now I'm not so sure."

"Does she do it to Phillip?"

"Not that I've noticed—but she sets Tamika off in a big way. Mika's still upset that we hired her."

"Maybe you need to think about getting rid of both of them."

Shea rested her wrist against her forehead. "How did things go so wrong so fast?"

"Just watch them, okay?"

Lightning crackled, and thunder boomed.

"Watch everyone."

She shivered as rain suddenly lashed against the window. It was hard and driving, relentless.

It was nothing compared to the look on Derek's face as he slid his T-shirt up over her hips.

"And not everything is going wrong," he said huskily. With a smooth move, he rolled on top of her and slid in deep. "Some things are finally very, very right."

The storm was in full swing when Shea finally made it into the office late that afternoon. Parking in her reserved spot, she looked up at the sky. Seeing a brief letup in the downpour, she reached for her umbrella and briefcase and made a mad dash to the door. Still, her skirt and shoes were damp when she made it inside.

"Shea!"

Looking up, she found the front office crowded. Almost simultaneously, a bolt of lightning lit the room. The faces of her employees were imprinted on her mind as clearly as if it had been photographic film.

Watch everyone.

Derek's words rang in her ears along with the crack of thunder that suddenly split the air.

"How's Phillip?" Tamika asked, rising from her seat behind her desk. "Was he really attacked?"

"We heard a news blip on the radio," Lynette said quickly. "Do they have any idea who did this?"

The barrage of questions was expected. The feelings of doubt and suspicion they raised were not.

"As best we can tell, he was mugged," Shea said, concentrating on her umbrella. Giving herself time, she shook the rain off it and hung it from the coatrack. "I just came from the hospital."

"Is he going to be all right?" asked Bruce, her operations manager.

"He's got a bad concussion." Wind rattled the windows as Shea crossed the room. She brushed more rain off her suit and ran a hand across her hair. "The doctors are planning to keep him overnight for observation, but they might be able to release him tomorrow."

"Does he need anything? What can we do?"

Shea looked at Tamika's face. The concern she saw there seemed real and unforced. "Just keep him in your thoughts."

"This is just so hard to believe," Bruce said.

"He didn't deserve this. Not *Phillip*," Lynette agreed. "At least he's in a good hospital. They treated my stepmother well. It's just so terrible he ended up there."

"I know," Shea said. It was all terrible. Terrible that her best friend had been hurt, terrible that she was looking at those closest to him with distrust. They all looked genuinely guileless.

Yet that made the hair on her arms raise even more.

"Should we be worried?"

Her head snapped toward Bruce.

He waved his clipboard at the parking lot. "First there was that prowler, and now Phillip's been attacked. Is something going on we should know about?"

Tamika and Lynette looked at each other wide-eyed.

"Mr. Oneiros did have his security team crawling all over the place today," Lynette said.

"You were the target!" Tamika said abruptly. "That's why Derek's people were here."

Shea felt a pull between her shoulder blades. "The Oneiros agency added some security measures as a precaution. The police are officially handling the investigation."

Unfortunately, as Derek had warned her, their scrutiny was now on her. Her fingers curled tightly around the handle of her briefcase. "I recommend that you all be careful. Now, let's concentrate on doing business. Phillip would hate it if we missed a sale because of him."

Bruce cleared his throat. "Well, I don't know if this is the right time to tell you, but we might have missed more than just a sale."

Shea looked at her operations manager. She really couldn't take much more bad news.

"With all the chaos here today, we ran behind. We didn't get that shipment of eye cream out to Cleveland. It's going to be late."

"How late?"

"A couple of days."

Thunder rumbled, and the vibrations ran up Shea's

feet. Biodermatics's lotions were their bread and butter. The income they generated paid her employees' salaries and allowed her the luxury to do the research she wanted to do. Was somebody trying to sabotage her entire company?

A chill ran down her spine.

Bruce continued. "If you've got a few minutes, we really need to talk about this new production schedule."

Production schedule?

He shook his head. "Things are only going to get worse if we switch to this."

"Let me see that." Shea took the clipboard and scanned the spreadsheet. With one glance, she knew that Phillip hadn't put this together. Neither had she. Her hand tightened. "Lynette, can I have a word with you in my office?"

Stiffly, Shea headed down the hallway. She heard Lynette follow at a much slower pace.

"Yes, Dr. Caldwell?" the woman asked when she finally stepped into the private office.

"What is this?" Shea asked, holding up the spreadsheet.

Lynette's face faltered. "I was alone this morning. Mr. Oneiros said I should do the best I could, and I knew that was something you'd been procrastinating about."

After eavesdropping outside Phillip's office?

Shea felt her cheeks flush with anger. "This is outside your authority. More importantly, it's wrong. If we tried running this fast, we'd risk machinery breakdowns and union problems."

"Oh, we would?"

Yes, they would! Not to mention that the overtime pay could put them out of business. Shea dropped her briefcase into her chair with a clatter. "Have you canceled Phillip's appointments?"

"Uh . . . no."

"Please do so."

Lynette folded her hands together. "I was just trying to help."

"I understand that." Shea held the schedule out to the woman. "But undo whatever you did here."

"*Undo?*"

"Tell Bruce we're going back to the old schedule until Phillip is back. Thank you."

Shea turned away. Unbelievable! How could she ever have considered leaving these people in charge of her company? She raked her hands through her hair. Maybe it was best that the earliest Dr. Wainright could get her into another sleep clinic was the end of next week.

And maybe it wasn't.

Feeling trapped, Shea walked over to the window and gripped the sill tightly. Rain beat against the windowpane, and she looked up at the sky. It was darker than ever. Night was battling day—and darkness was winning.

"Shea?" The soft voice came from the doorway. "Are you okay?"

She tore her gaze away from the Dumpster across the way. "I'm fine."

Tamika crossed the room. "Don't let Lynette bother you. I can handle her."

Shea raked a hand through her hair. "I'm just really on edge right now."

"That's understandable." Reaching out, Tamika rubbed her shoulder. "I know how close you and Phillip are."

"You're close to him, too."

"You found him, didn't you?"

The words were like an icy trickle going down Shea's spine. "How do you know that?"

"The news reporter said it happened at your complex."

"Where were you this morning?" Shea blurted. At the narrowing of her assistant's eyes, she folded her arms around her waist. "Derek said you were out. I could have used you here."

Tamika hesitated, the toe of one shoe twisting against the floor. "If you must know, I went to the bank to get a loan. I took vacation time."

Shea frowned. "Are you having problems?"

"No. I just decided I needed something."

She walked over to the window to gaze out at the storm. Shea turned with her, intending to dig deeper, but her questions froze in her throat. She'd just gotten a good look at her assistant's shoes.

"I feel so bad for Phillip," Tamika said quietly.

Shea couldn't respond. All she could see were the black-and-white, zebra-striped stilettos on Tamika's feet. They were nearly identical to her shoes, the ones that she'd found pointing toward her drenched kitchen window the morning after she'd sleepwalked.

Oh, God. *Had* her Somnambulist been trying to tell her something?

Tamika rocked back onto her heel, pointing the toe of that crazy shoe into the air. "You just never think that something like this will happen to someone you know."

"No," Shea said. "You never really do."

"It's scary."

Thunder rolled.

"Yes, it is."

Fourteen

The Somnambulist waited forever for his beloved to fall asleep that night. He floated back and forth across her window, watching as she rolled and turned from one side of the bed to the other. Something had perturbed her.

Was it the lightning and thunder? He liked storms. He got off on the swirling and the howling, the sizzling energy. He loved the smell of burnt air, and the *whoosh* of pressure that rolled through him with every crack. It made his particles hum.

But not as much as she did.

He waited anxiously, raindrops falling through him, as his She-a settled into unconsciousness. Still, he didn't enter the room. He felt twitchy. Wreaker stench was in the air. There was one nearby—or had been—but the creature hadn't seen him.

He sniffed harder, and the musky scent of her lotion tickled his senses. He swayed in delight. It was the yummy stuff that made her skin so soft, so supple and smooth. It made him ache to be inside her. He wanted to *feel*.

Anger made his fragments thrum. Where was he, that peeking Wreaker? It was the one with the mean eyes; he knew it. "Third wheel. Glom-on-er."

Instinct told him he should leave. Greed made him stay.

He didn't need to be here tonight; he felt strong and fast. She'd done that for him. Last night they'd been strong together, faster than the wind. He could still feel the stairs pounding under her feet, hear the startled exclamation of their visitor and smell the scent of fear.

It had excited him. He wanted more.

Annoyed, the Somnambulist let his toe slide through the wall and into the bedroom. Tempted beyond caution, he slipped into the room and waited, tensed, as his molecules reassembled. All was quiet. He floated closer. Paused. A little closer. Finally, he was suspended by his She-a's bed.

"Pretty girl. Smart girl."

She'd known what to do when he'd finally shown her the face in the window.

He bounced up over her, extended himself to her length, and slowly lowered himself into her. "Mmmm," he purred as he stretched.

Her body extended right along with him.

"Hm?" He pointed her toes. She was lighter tonight, free-flowing. The cobwebs had cleared from her head. He'd made her better! The Dream Wreakers' hold on her had been broken.

Blew them away, he had! Like a match to a fuse. TNT to dust.

Excitement made him flutter, and he saw her nightie quiver. Lifting her hand, he caressed the pretty gown. It was soft and slick.

He knew someplace else that was soft and slick. Oh, the secret she'd shown him!

Pinching the material between her thumb and forefinger, he lifted her head and peeked underneath. There were those red berries. Hissing with eagerness, he slipped her hand underneath her nightie and gave one of the pink bumps a pinch.

Her breath exhaled in a puff, and her body jumped.

There it was, the power and the exhilarating rush.

Shoving the material aside, he slipped her other hand in. He squeezed and tugged, scratched and rolled. Her bottom squiggled on the mattress, and that hungry heat filled her belly.

"My She-a! My lovely princess." He hummed inside her, luxuriating in her. They'd walk farther tonight. He'd loved the prickle of grass under her feet and the brush of wind against her skin. What would the rain feel like? He could only imagine that cold dampness splattering across her—

What was that?

He lifted her head off the pillow with a jerk.

Was that a noise? Downstairs? He curled her lips into a snarl.

He thought they'd run them off, chased them away. Why couldn't the interlopers leave them alone?

Pulling her hands away from those feel-good bumps, he bounced her from the bed. He looked around for something hard; he knew how to stop this now. Wrapping her fingers around the lamp beside the bed, he tore the plug out of the wall and stomped toward the door. He pulled it open with a *whoosh* and—

"Wreaker!"

It was standing right in front of him with its mean eyes glaring.

Pain scorched the Somnambulist, too much to enjoy. That hand of death came at him, and he lurched back. He jumped right out of his She-a's body and dispersed, just pulled apart and disappeared.

Still, the fingers seared him and he screamed.

Shea came awake so fast, it felt as if sleep was being torn from her, just ripped away. She gasped for air and clenched at the doorjamb. A scream rang in her head.

Had she made that sound?

Footsteps pounded. Lightning lit up the room and, this time, she knew her scream was her own. It ripped through her vocal cords and hurt her ears. Someone was standing right in front of her!

"Shea!"

The figure caught her firmly by the shoulders. Her entire body shuddered when those strong hands gave her a hard shake.

"Shea! It's me. Wake up."

She blinked, confused. "Derek?"

Reaching into the room, he hit the light switch. Light flooded behind her, but it was muted compared to the harsh flash that had frightened her before. That didn't make the picture any easier to bear. She found herself standing in her doorway, with no idea how she'd gotten there.

A weight pulled at her hand. Looking at it, she gasped.

Her lamp clattered to the floor, smashing and sending sharp glass flying.

Derek jumped out of the way and pulled her out into the hallway and into the shadows. Shea pulled back worriedly. The light from the bedroom cast a rectangle on the far wall, but outside of that everything was pitch-black.

What had just happened?

"Are you all right?" he asked.

She looked into his dark eyes. "Are you?"

They both glanced at the shards on the floor.

"I'm fine," he said. "You're the one who's shaking."

So she was. He pulled her closer, and she went to him instinctively. He felt strong and whole. She could see he wasn't hurt—but he could have been. If she'd hit him with that lamp—

"This means nothing." His voice was low and firm. "Don't read anything into this."

"It's spelled out pretty clearly, don't you think?" She couldn't stop looking at the glass and metal on the floor. This was exactly what she'd been afraid would happen. This was why she'd wanted him anywhere but here.

"We've got to get you warmed up. Stay here."

Shivering, she watched as he carefully stepped around the broken glass. She had to get him to leave.

She needed to leave. She'd go sit on the sleep clinic's doorstep until they took her in.

"Here," Derek said, appearing in front of her again. "Put this on."

He had her robe. She stuck her arms into the sleeves as he tied the belt securely around her waist. Catching her by the lapels, he made her look at him. "Don't even think about it. I'm not going anywhere. If you had let me sleep with you, you never would have made it off the bed."

She wasn't so sure. "I need a drink," she said hoarsely, and walked unsteadily down the hallway.

His footsteps followed close behind. "What about the sleeping pills?"

"I stopped taking them." They hadn't worked, had they?

Nothing was working!

She slapped the light switch at the top of the stairs. Her knees felt wobbly, and she took the steps one at a time. When she started to cross the living room, her steps slowed further. "Did we leave a light on?"

Derek looked over her shoulder. "Not that I remember."

The kitchen light was wavering, flickering.

Shea's skin pulled tight. That wasn't a bad bulb. She knew what that was.

Lifting up the hem of her robe, she ran across the room. She spun into the kitchen, but stopped so fast, her knees nearly went out from under her.

"Oh, God," she said, fighting for air. "Oh, God. No!"

Derek skidded in behind her. "Oh, shit!"

Everywhere Shea looked, candles were glowing. Candles on the counter. Candles on the chairs. Candles on the floor. The acrid smell of fire filled her nose and choked her throat.

She let out a cry and dove for the one nearest her. Blowing fiercely, she tried to put out the flame. Clapping her hand atop the bell jar next to it, she robbed that fire of oxygen. She whirled around to tackle the next.

"Careful," Derek snapped. He caught her arm and tried to pull her back.

Fighting back her fear, she ventured deeper into the room. Fire jumped all around her. Her air was coming in and out of her lungs so fast, she didn't know if she had any to spare.

She started blowing anyway.

"Go back," he said. "I'll take care of it."

She spun. There were more on the table. Tea lights. Oil lamps. Candles in jars and pillars. Votives.

"It's all right. They're under control. Just let me put them out before—"

A taper candle was burning too closely to the paper towels under her cabinets. She turned fast, and her robe billowed.

Derek roared.

Everything happened in a blur. He caught her by the shoulders and started yanking her clothes off her. He was yelling at her, but she only caught pieces of what he was saying. "On fire," rang in her ears.

She knew the room was on fire! She tried to pull

away from him to help, but his grip turned rough. She heard her robe tear, then he threw it into the sink. Wide-eyed, she watched as he turned on the faucet and doused the material.

She'd been on fire.

"Get out," he ordered. He pushed her toward the living room. "Get out!"

She stumbled back and watched, terrified, as Derek went back into the room.

Oh, God. She couldn't let him go back in there.

She reached out to pull him back, but even in her terror, she noticed how in control he was. And how smoke wasn't burning her eyes . . .

Slowly, she realized that it wasn't as bad as she'd thought. Those sinuous flames made her want to recoil, but she made herself look closer. Each of them came from a wick. This wasn't a conflagration. The room wasn't engulfed.

A pinch here and a puff there, and soon the room was dark.

But it was too late; the fear had already taken root. Shea couldn't contain it. She backed away and bumped into the back of the couch. She gripped it with both hands.

Her chest . . . It hurt. She couldn't breathe. She wanted to scream.

Derek came out of the kitchen, his eyes hard. His jaw was rigid and his fists were clenched. The light from the stairs lit him jaggedly, emphasizing the shadows that surrounded them.

The shadows that liked to play with her . . .

Shea rubbed her breastbone with the ball of her hand. Her heart felt like it was going to burst from her chest.

It had happened again. The unthinkable had happened again!

"It's out." He approached her carefully, as if she were a wild animal. "It's gone."

"It's not gone!" she said, her throat tight. "It's *back*. It's back, and it's inside me."

He stopped, his hand lifted toward her. "What's inside you?"

"The thing that did *that*."

He shook his head. "You didn't do that."

She rocked back and forth. She couldn't take this. She couldn't. "Yes, I did. It likes fire. It's dangerous. *I'm* dangerous."

Derek looked confused and concerned. God, he must think she'd totally lost it.

"Shea, somebody else did this. Somebody got into your house again. We need to call the police."

She laughed, the sound humorless. "The same somebody who left the footprints? The somebody who hit Phillip over the head? Face it, I nearly attacked you!"

"You never made it out your bedroom door. Somebody got in, somebody who knows you're afraid of fire. Who has keys?"

She shook her head. He didn't understand. Couldn't.

"Check the cameras!" He pointed at the one in the living room, but cursed when he realized it had been pointed at the stairs, not the kitchen. Fingers biting, he caught her by the shoulders. "Listen to me. You didn't light those candles."

"Yes, I did. It's just like before."

"You don't even keep them in the house."

"It doesn't matter. I would have found a way."

"What are you talking about?"

"This isn't the first time this has happened! I started that fire in our trailer when I was little. I was sleepwalking then, too."

There it was, the nasty, festering secret she'd been keeping for years.

Yet letting it out didn't make her feel any better. The words felt bitter against her tongue. It made her want to be sick.

"Oh, fuck," Derek breathed, looking at her in horror.

She knew why; she could barely look at herself. Still, his reaction hurt.

She tensed as he pulled her into his arms and buried his face in her hair. How could he touch her? How could he stand to be anywhere near her?

"What happened?" he asked against her ear.

She shuddered. She'd never wanted to relive this again, but here she was looking at wisps of smoke coming out of her kitchen and waiting for the smoke detectors to start wailing.

"Tell me."

She swallowed hard around the lump in her throat. "I . . . I woke up outside. I was lying in the ditch. The lights and sirens roused me."

Her eyes stung as if she'd gone back in time.

"The flames, they were so big. They reached up so high into the night sky, and things started popping." She flinched as the ugly sounds echoed in her ears. "I couldn't find my dad. He wasn't anywhere I looked, but Mrs. Lupescu saw me. She . . . She crossed herself against me and ran. That's when I knew."

"No," Derek said, pulling back to look into her face. "I read about that fire. The results of the investigation were inconclusive. Nobody knows what started it."

"I know. The Somnambulist did it."

He stilled. "What did you say?"

He was going to think she was crazy, but it was what she'd been told as a child. She was older now; she knew the laws of physics and the nature of science. Deep down, though, it didn't make a difference. She knew what was true. She knew it as well as she knew her own name.

"A Somnambulist," she said, daring him to challenge her. "Mrs. Lupescu told me I was hexed. She told me that an evil spirit lived within me at night, making me do bad things. She was right. *I'm possessed.*"

She lurched away from him. "It lit the fire. I lit the fire. It makes no difference. My dad was almost killed because of me. He went back into that trailer to find me, and he'll bear the scars for the rest of his life."

Her words hung in the air as, suddenly, the room went quiet. Too quiet. The storm had moved on. It only made the sound of her breaths harsher. She and Derek stood apart, staring at each other. His look was laserlike. Unreadable.

"You think I need help," she whispered.

"Yes, I do."

His words felt like a smack in the face. Still, she nodded. "It would probably be for the best. They'll have to take me there. I'll . . . I'll check myself in."

She looked down at the ice-blue nightie she wore. It was the same one she'd been wearing when he'd crashed in her front door and made love to her. "Just let me change."

"No."

"I can't go like this."

"You're not going anywhere."

"But—"

"Mrs. Lupescu was right."

Shea watched Derek warily, not sure she'd heard him correctly. "Right about what?"

"You *are* possessed. You have a Somnambulist. I saw it."

The moment the words left his lips, Derek knew he'd jumped into the deep end. He'd never confessed his abilities to any human before, but she needed to know. He couldn't let her think she was going crazy. Or that she'd nearly killed her own father.

"I can't believe how that woman played with your head, but she was right," he said, his voice like gravel. "You have a parasite, and it's called a Somnambulist."

Shea's lips trembled. "Please, Derek. Don't do this."

He took a step toward her. "They only stay with their hosts for short periods of time, long enough to gather strength. I nearly had yours just now, but it got away."

She took a step back. "I know you think you're help-ing, but—"

"I'm not trying to mollify you. I'm telling you I can stop it."

She hesitated. "How?"

"You know how. I've told you." His heart thudded. "I'm an Oneiros—in every sense of the word."

Her eyes widened, but then it was as if she dissolved from the top down. Her eyelids closed, her shoulders slumped, and her hands fell limply at her sides. "Oh, my God."

Desperation filled Derek. Going at her fast, he backed her up against the sofa. He had to convince her now, get her to trust her heart over her mind or he would lose her. She tried to hold him off, but he pressed his body tightly against hers until heat coursed between them.

"I'm not trying to scare you. Just listen to me."

His heart was beating like a bass drum, but he kept his touch gentle as he intertwined their fingers. "People need me to help them dream. They go through the other sleep stages naturally, but that only repairs their bodies. I deal with the mind. It's my job to bring the human consciousness into the dream realm—my world."

The empathy in her blue eyes nearly broke him. She thought he was as unstable as she was. *The Somnambu-list*, he thought, his brain working fast. If she believed in it, why couldn't she believe in him?

"You've studied mythology. You know that most leg-ends are born in truth."

She inhaled shakily, and her breasts rubbed against

his chest. He kept the contact flush. He had to keep her close, off balance. It was the only way he was going to get through.

"My mother's name is Nyx. I have an army of brothers. I knew you were having sleep problems the moment you stepped into my office that day. Do you need me to go on?"

He could practically see the cogs in her brain turning. "What did I dream tonight?" she asked, challenging him.

"You didn't. It got to you first."

She went still. "Then last night."

She needed proof; he could give her that. "You finally found a place to put that carbon element on your magic molecule."

Her jaw went slack.

"I assume that had something to do with your research?"

She ignored the question. "The night before that," she said, her voice coming back strong.

A slow smile pulled at his lips. "Well, now, that would be the night you dreamed of the two of us in your laboratory."

The color drained from her face.

"I believe I had you bent over your lab bench." Deliberately, he pressed his hips against hers. "Your lab coat was thrown over your head as I—"

She pushed at his shoulders. "How do you *know* these things?"

"I'm your Dream Wreaker." He looked at her steadily,

needing her to take that leap of faith. "I can make it better, Shea. Somnambulists are my natural enemy. If anyone's going to get rid of that thing, it's going to be me."

She took a measured breath, and then another.

"I can help you."

She shook her head. "Just because I'm crazy doesn't mean you have to be."

"Neither of us is crazy."

"Why are you doing this?" she whispered. "Why are you telling me these things?"

"Because you need to know." But he knew it went deeper than that. "And because I love you."

Fifteen

Derek held the door to the restaurant open for Shea. As she passed, his hand automatically settled at the small of her back. Although she didn't stiffen, she still somehow managed to pull away.

His fingers curled in toward his palms.

Things between them had been strained ever since last night.

Neither of them seemed to know what to say or how to act. They'd both confessed to things that they weren't sure they wanted the other to know; now it was too late to pull the secrets back.

Honestly, he didn't want to.

Shea paused ahead of him, uncertain which way to go. Wordlessly, he pointed toward the back. She started moving in that direction, and he fell in step behind her. Unchecked, his gaze swept down her sleek body. She was wearing a tank top that showed off her velvety skin and a long, flowing skirt—the kind that made men wonder if she was just as soft underneath. With her blond hair brushing against her shoulders, she looked fresh and feminine, seductive as hell.

This had to work.

Her steps paused, and she glanced over her shoulder. She still couldn't quite meet his eyes. "Are we having breakfast with your brothers?"

"Yes."

"Who are the others with them?"

"They're all my brothers." The full local family contingent was here, except for Mack, who was on day duty. If Derek was going to do this, he wanted to face them all at once.

Going through the buzz saw twice didn't appeal to him.

Taking the surprise in stride, Shea headed to the table.

"Tony," she said in greeting. "Cael."

Zane pulled out a chair for her, and she slid into it gracefully. "Thank you. Good morning."

Introductions were made. As always, his brothers reverted to their best behavior with a beautiful woman around. Still, Derek could already feel the sidelong looks drilling into him.

"When did we start letting girls join?" Zane asked, a smile on his face.

"Today, apparently," came a smooth female voice. "You have a problem with that?"

Zane's head snapped up, and his smile broadened when he saw the woman standing over their table with one hand propped saucily on her hip. "Not at all. How you doin', Sexy Red?"

Cael glowered at their younger brother. "Her name is Devon." Standing, he hooked an arm around his girlfriend's waist and gave her a quick but heated kiss. "What are you doing here?"

"Derek invited me." Her eyes sparked with interest when she noticed Shea. "Hi, I'm Devon Bradshaw."

"Shea Caldwell. Nice to meet you."

Derek drummed his fingers against the tabletop as seats were switched and room was made for their latest arrival. He could feel Cael's curiosity and irritation, but his brother could grumble all he wanted. He'd asked Devon here for moral support: Shea's *and* his.

"Hi, guys," Sally said, hurrying up to their table. Looking rushed, she stuffed her order pad into her apron and passed out menus like a Vegas poker dealer. "What are you doing here on a Saturday? This is our busy morning. Sorry I won't be able to chat today."

"We're wounded," Zane said, pouting.

"Yeah, like you don't get enough female attention." She winked at the newcomers. "Can I take your drink orders?"

Derek looked around uncertainly. Now that they were here, he didn't know if it really was the right place for this discussion. IHOP *was* hopping, and having so many ears around made him edgy.

He didn't need the added strain.

As normal as his brothers were trying to act, they

were exchanging looks. Chairs were shifting, and muscles were tensing. Shea wasn't immune to the mood. Her hands knotted in her lap as she sat quietly, not moving.

"Derek?" Sally said.

He almost jumped. "Uh, water. Water is fine."

He reached to straighten his tie. His hand fumbled when there wasn't one around his neck. Instead, he rubbed his palm against his jeans. God, he felt like he was getting ready to jump off a cliff.

Sally left, but nobody at the table was thinking about food. All eyes were on him.

Finally, Shea asked the question that was on everyone's mind. "Why are we here, Derek?"

He braced himself, but then just let go. "We're here because I need you to know I was telling you the truth. There's a reason our last name is Oneiros."

Not one of his brothers moved. No one even blinked at the unexploded bombshell he'd dropped. Still, he could feel the atmosphere building like a pressure cooker.

His gaze swept over the stoic faces. "She believes in Somnambulists, and she knows she has one."

"Derek." Reaching out, Shea caught his arm.

Her grip was tight, and she'd paled to the color of chalk. She looked like she wanted to flay him for revealing what she considered a humiliating secret, her belief in nighttime monsters.

He barreled ahead anyway.

"It's getting worse, and she needs to know we can help her. That *I* can help her."

Silence greeted him from all sides, and the tinkle of laughter from surrounding tables rubbed against his nerves.

Finally Tony started fiddling with his silverware. It was the only movement at the table. "Did something else happen that we don't know about?"

"The Somnie took another walk with her."

"With you in the place?" Zane blurted. He caught a startled look from Shea and sank deeper into his seat.

"Yes, with me there." Derek's knee began to bounce under the table. Somebody needed to step up, or she was going to be through with him. The little parlor tricks with her dreams weren't going to be enough to hold her.

"She studied Greek mythology in college," he said. "I told her that the myths about us are true—that we are the real Oneiroi."

This time, the reactions couldn't be avoided. Tony dropped his fork, and it rang like a bell. Wes tilted onto the back legs of his chair, and AJ cursed out loud.

Shea looked around the table uncertainly. Derek knew she thought he'd been trying to placate her with his stories and claims. Just one word, just the slightest bit of confirmation would help.

He searched his brothers' faces. He'd just committed their greatest sin. He'd exposed them, and right in the middle of a crowded restaurant. But she was important to him, too, more so every day. Couldn't somebody just—

"He wasn't supposed to tell you that."

Derek's head snapped toward the voice, right along with Shea's. It was Cael. Cael, their leader.

"But it's true," his older brother said. "We are Dream Wreakers."

"Thank God," Devon whispered. She caught her lover's hand.

Cael's stern features softened as he turned to Shea. "What do you need to know, Dr. Caldwell?"

Dumbfounded, Shea looked around the table. Gazes were quickly diverted. Fingers thrummed and a spoon twirled. Yet as she waited, nobody denied what had been said. "Dream Wreakers?" she said tentatively.

"It's a loose translation of the Greek 'Oneiroi,'" Cael explained.

The pulse at her temple fluttered. Derek could see she was torn between disbelief and wanting to ask questions. His own heart began to pound a little faster.

"I thought you lived on the shores in a cave near Hades," she teased. She clearly wanted to laugh this all off.

"We integrated into society a while ago." Cael's tone turned dry. "The commute was a bitch."

Shea's responding smile was nervous and unsure. "And the black wings?"

"Ugh. Those stinking wings." Zane slung his arm over the back of his chair. "I mean, really—did those scribes have to go and make us ugly? At least Hermes only got tiny ones on his feet."

"Zane," Wes hissed.

Shea stared at Zane with astonishment. His disdain

for the myth was obvious, and as counterintuitive as that was, it made it more believable.

"Sorry," he said, catching her look. "I just—"

"Can you read minds?" she blurted.

Derek shot a surprised look at her. She *had* been trying to figure out how he could see into her dreams.

Zane blushed—actually blushed. "Only when the person is dreaming," he mumbled.

Giving in to her scientist's need for answers, Shea leaned forward and asked quietly, "How do you do it? How do you manage sleepers' thoughts? How do you decide what dreams they'll have?"

Tony stopped twirling his knife between his fingers and pointed it at her. "That's another misconception."

He blinked, surprised at his own outburst. Shea pinned him with a look, though. Uncomfortable, Tony set down the knife and aligned it precisely with the rest of his silverware. "Sorry, but that's one of my pet peeves. We *can* lead dreams, but we try not to. We just get you going—prime the pump."

"But how?" she insisted.

Everyone looked at one another.

Cael finally answered. "Suffice it to say we don't sleep like normal people."

"Oh, tell her," Devon said sharply. She threw Shea a shrewd look. "They have magic hands—but you already know that."

Derek watched Shea flush, yet her eyes were bright.

"They can control brain waves with their fingertips,"

Devon continued. "They lead sleepers out of the deepest stage and into REM."

"How do they get to people, though?" Shea asked. "They're sleeping in locked houses."

"By astral projecting: they split themselves in two."

Cael shifted uncomfortably when a busboy passed their table. "That's simplifying it quite a bit."

"It's the easiest way to describe it, and none of you have seen yourselves do it." Devon brushed her auburn hair over her shoulder. "It's unnerving. Their spirit literally separates and goes into the dream realm."

Shea drew back slowly. "Leaving their bodies in a sleep that looks like a coma?"

"Yes." Devon fought off a shudder. "Just like that."

Derek suddenly felt Shea's touch, and under the table, her fingers intertwined with his. The knot in his chest loosened. Gripping her tightly, he settled their joined hands onto his thigh.

"And Somnambulists?" she asked.

Finally, she was looking at him. Finally, she was talking to him.

"They're real, too," he said quietly.

"But you can get rid of them?"

"I can."

"How?"

He hesitated. "That's why we're here. I need to talk to my brothers and make a plan."

Devon got the message. Reaching down, she caught her purse. "Let's go powder our noses, Shea."

"But I want to help."

Derek shook his head. "This is something we have to do without you."

"But I know this thing better than any of you."

"And it knows you." He let his voice drop so it was only the two of them. "It can tap into your consciousness, Curie. How do you think it knew Phillip's phone number?"

"Oh," she breathed, understanding dawning. "Oh, God."

"It can't know when we're coming, or how."

She swallowed hard, then nodded. "We'll take our time."

Derek rose and helped her with her chair. More than one man glanced up as the two women headed toward the restroom. He didn't blame them; they were beautiful—but they *were* taken.

A calm came over him. His brothers could do whatever they wanted to him. He didn't care. The risk had been worth it.

Still, the shots started coming before he even sat back down.

"What do you think you're doing?" Tony's arms bunched as he braced his elbows on the table. "We're not supposed to talk about things like that in front of people. She's a liability now."

"I had to," Derek said. "And she won't say anything."

"You don't know that," Tony replied.

"Yes, I do. She's good at keeping secrets." Too good, in Derek's opinion. If she'd told him earlier about the sleepwalking or that she believed in the supernatural, he might have been able to do something. "Besides, she's a well-respected scientist. Talking about us wouldn't help her professional reputation."

"But did you *have* to tell her?" Tony asked. "Why not work it from the other side, like we usually do? Just cleave the Somnambulist from her and be done with it?"

"Because this thing is out of control—and so is her stalker."

Tony's face fell. "Oh, shit. What happened now?"

Derek raked a hand across his face. "Somebody got into her condo last night and lit a bunch of candles. Shea lost it; she thought she'd set the kitchen on fire while she was sleepwalking. She was talking about committing herself. I *had* to tell her, so she wouldn't think she was crazy. It was the only way to settle her down."

"She's terrified of fire." Zane looked around at all the questioning faces. "Something like that would have messed her up big time."

The mood turned somber. Things got even more quiet when Sally showed up with their drinks.

Cael waited until she was out of earshot, then leaned in close. "This person obviously knows her. How did they get in?"

"The door," Derek said. He'd already changed the locks. "Phillip had her backup key."

"Any idea who it is?" Cael asked.

"I have concerns about some of her employees." Derek glanced at Zane. "Was Tamika sleeping around midnight last night?"

Zane grimaced. "She didn't call for me until almost two o'clock. It's almost like she's not sleeping on purpose."

"Tamika Hendricks?" AJ's head snapped up. "What are you doing with her?"

Zane shrugged. "Derek traded her for Shea. She's my charge now."

"The hell you say!" AJ glared across the table. "I'm watching for her in the day; it's only fair I should get the night work."

Derek made a chopping motion with his hand. "What about Lynette Fromm? Tony, don't you have her?"

"Lynette who?"

"Fromm."

"Oh, yeah. She's one of mine."

"How's she been sleeping?"

Tony scratched his chin. "She sleeps in patches. Her brain wave patterns have always been all over the place. I really couldn't tell you when she got to bed last night. Sorry; I've got a lot of charges."

"Right." Derek ran his thumb over the lip of his glass of water. "Right."

"What is it?" Cael asked.

"The Somnambulist," Derek said softly. "I don't like how deep it's gotten its claws into Shea."

"Did you see it last night?" Wes asked curiously. Like Zane, he was young and hadn't dealt with an adult of the species.

"I nearly had it. I singed it, but it's fast. Real fast."

"What do you want to do about it?" Cael asked. "I know you already have a plan."

Derek took a deep breath. "I think we need to make some changes. "I need to be on Shea 24/7."

Zane snorted. "That's obvious."

Derek nailed him with a look. "She's got threats coming at her from all angles. If I'm going to protect her, I need to be there for her full time. It's a lot to ask, I know, but I need all of you to cover my other charges until I get this thing. It's obsessed with her."

"Do you really think it will come back?" Cael asked. "Now that it knows you're close to her?"

"It'll be back. It might lay low for a while, but it will be back. And I'll be waiting."

"You can't."

Derek glanced sharply at his older brother.

Cael raked a hand through his hair. "Not if you want to get rid of it for good."

"He's right." Tony crossed his arms over his chest. "If you stand guard over her, it will stay just out of your reach, hounding you, waiting for you to make a slip."

"I'll get it," Derek growled.

"This is not a game of tag," Cael said sternly. "The best way to catch it is to back off. You need to let the Somnie think that she's vulnerable, that you've left her to him."

"What are you saying?" Zane sat forward, his fists clenched nearly as tightly as Derek's. "He's *supposed* to let it get her?"

A muscle tugged in Cael's jaw. "That's exactly what I'm saying."

Tony nodded. "Let it overtake her."

Derek's neck began to ache. "I can't do that." He

knew how petrified she was of the thing. He'd just told her he could protect her!

"You have to," Cael said quietly. His head turned slowly. "Because as soon as it's occupied and distracted, you're going to go in for the kill."

The table fell silent once again.

"Don't miss this time," Tony warned. "You might not get another chance."

The ache in Derek's neck spread to his shoulders and down his arms. He had to get it; this thing had been terrorizing her for years. It had made her do unbearable things. She couldn't take much more. It was up to him to finish it.

"I'll take on as many of your charges as you need," Zane said. "Save your girl."

Derek looked across the table in surprise. "Thanks," he said gruffly.

Tony held up a hand. "Don't worry, D-man. Your charges will be covered."

As one, his brothers nodded.

Heads at surrounding tables started turning again, and Derek saw two bombshells, one redhead and one blonde, making their way back across the room.

Cael's gaze honed in on Devon. "Are you sure you don't need any backup?"

Derek watched as Shea came toward him. "No. That son of a bitch is mine."

Breakfast had been . . . memorable. Shea wondered what had gone on at the table when she and Devon had left, but she had a feeling she'd never find out.

At least things had calmed down when they'd returned, and she'd enjoyed meeting Derek's brothers and future sister-in-law immensely.

Yet as she watched him sliding a shiny key into the new lock on her front door, her agitation returned. Her gaze slid up from his sure hands to his muscled arms and shoulders.

Her home opened, welcoming them, and Derek stepped back. His gaze landed on her as it had so many times before, hot and searching. She stepped over the threshold and felt his hand touch the small of her back.

This time she didn't shy away.

"Thank you for breakfast. I like your brothers a lot." She heard the door close as she tossed her purse onto the couch.

Derek stood behind her, his body tense. "Do you believe me now? Do you understand what we are? What we—"

She turned around and kissed him. She understood a lot. He had a family that loved him.

"I missed you," she said, sliding her hands up around his neck.

His arms came around her. "God, I missed you, too."

She went up on her tiptoes, kissing him harder and sliding her tongue deep. She felt his cock press against her belly, instantly hardening, but he pulled back.

"Do you believe me?"

She chose her words carefully. "My mind is open."

The things she'd been told were fantastical, but he

and his brothers clearly believed them. Either they were all in on the game, or there had to be some truth hidden in there somewhere.

And who was she to point fingers? She had beliefs that couldn't be proven. Early scientists hadn't believed Copernicus when he'd claimed the earth was round— and Einstein had postulated on the existence of parallel universes.

"Good enough for me."

Derek's head dipped, and his body enveloped hers. Shea felt heat and relief pour through her. Last night had been terrible, the distance between them almost worse than what had happened to create it. She'd missed being able to trust him.

She wanted him back.

"Make love to me," she whispered.

He started nudging her toward the sofa, but she dug in her heels.

"The kitchen."

His mouth stilled against her neck. "Are you sure?"

"Yes." She didn't want to be thinking about flames every time she walked in there.

"Show me my dream, Oneiros," she said impulsively. "Pretend that table is my lab bench."

He took the dare without missing a beat.

Half-carrying, half-pushing her, he stumbled into the room. Shea wasn't any more patient. She tugged Derek's T-shirt out of his jeans and reached under it to caress his rock-hard abs. He crowded her further, and her butt bumped against the table.

His mouth was voracious, and so were his hands. Her tank top stretched as he yanked it over her head, then he was kissing her again.

"I'll protect you," he said as his fingers went to the clasp of her bra.

"And I'll protect your secret." Desperately, she yanked at his T-shirt. He pulled it over his head and caught her waist. The room spun as he turned her around. The underwire of her bra bit into her ribs as he fought with the hooks at the back.

"Damn it." Finally, he jerked it hard and the hooks gave way.

Shea's nipples stiffened as he peeled the straps down her arms. Her bra fell onto her foot, and then his hands were on her, taking possession. He cupped her breasts and massaged them hard, his fingers pinching at the tender tips.

"Ohhh," she groaned, her head falling back against his shoulder.

Their bodies swayed together as he worked her good. Frantically, she gripped his thighs. His hips pressed forward, and he ground his stiff cock against her butt.

Openmouthed kisses ran down her neck, and Shea trembled. One of Derek's hands left her breast and skimmed down her stomach. She groaned when it slid purposefully between her legs and cupped her.

"Bend over," he whispered into her ear.

The delicious words had her creaming right into his palm. Could he feel that? With her skirt and panties in the way?

"Bend. Over."

He nipped at her neck and need exploded inside her. Obeying, she bent at the waist. Reaching in front of her, he pushed aside the centerpiece and a napkin holder.

The candles were long gone. She'd thrown them all into a garbage bag last night. Still . . .

"Lie flat."

The order kicked the memory right out of her head—as she suspected it was meant to do—and she obeyed.

His hand settled between her shoulder blades, his fingers spread wide. "Do you want it like in the dream?"

Oh, God. He really could see into her head.

"Yes," she whispered.

Her breasts pressed flat against the cold wood, making her nipples ache. That just made it all the better. She pressed herself down harder, flattening the tips as Derek's hands fisted in her skirt.

"You know," he said, his voice raspy. "This table could double as my desk."

Her pussy squeezed. He'd had the same fantasy she had.

Her muscles tightened as he gathered the material of her skirt. Every brush of his fingers, every drag of his knuckles . . . She was nearly out of her mind when he draped the skirt over her waist. Her brain flashed crystal clear, though, when he dropped to his knees behind her.

Shea quickly looked over her shoulder. All she could see were his hands pulling at her bikini bottoms. That, and the top of his head . . .

Oh, dear Lord.

Turning her face into the table, she pressed her forehead against the surface.

"So pretty," he murmured as he peeled her underwear down, down, down . . .

The air felt cool as it hit her exposed flesh. Shea's fingernails scraped against the tabletop, but she went still as hot breaths puffed against her.

"Derek," she groaned.

"So soft."

His hands slid down the backs of her thighs, all the way to her feet.

"Spread."

A cry left her lips as pressure started pushing her feet outward. Her sandals slipped on the slick floor, and her heel hooked her bra strap. He didn't stop. Wider and wider he took her, until her toes bumped into the legs of the table.

"All right?" he asked softly.

"Yes." She was *so* turned on.

"All right."

His breaths were right against her. Her pussy felt like it was on fire. Yet still, he didn't touch her there.

His hands slid from her ankles to her feet. "Let's get these off of you."

Shea kicked at her shoes. Off, on, she didn't care. She just wanted—

"Ah!"

Her entire body jerked when his tongue stroked over her, raspy and wet.

She wanted *that.*

The pleasure was sharp and intense. His hands tightened on her ankles. His mouth went at her more aggressively, and she let out a long groan.

"Ohhh. Oh, Derek!"

He was licking at her, nipping at her sensitive folds. Just when she got used to the sensation, he switched it up and began sucking on her clit.

Biting her lip, she looked over her shoulder. His hair brushed against her bottom, and his face was buried in her cunny. His tongue suddenly plunged into her, and her body clenched.

"Fuck," Derek said, the forced calm gone.

Standing abruptly, he began tearing at his jeans.

Shea rocked back against him. She was close, so close.

"Fuck," he repeated, his breathing harsh. In one swoop, he pushed down his briefs and jeans together. They hit him mid-thigh as he reached out and caught her hips.

Shea reached back for him, her hands searching.

Her fingers flexed when he thrust into her hard, and her cry echoed off the kitchen walls.

He bent over her, his chest hot against her back and his zipper digging into her thighs. "If you'll let me, I'll make all your dreams come true."

His hands covered hers. Finger by finger, he wrapped them around the edge of the table near her hips. Shea moaned. He had her trapped, her breasts pressed flat and his cock buried deep.

"Please," she pleaded. "Take me."

"One more detail."

Easing up, he caught her skirt again. Her heart jumped. The polished walnut tabletop beneath her suddenly clouded with condensation from her harsh breaths. She knew what he was going to do, but she didn't know if she really wanted . . .

He spread the material wide and tossed it over her. It fluttered, catching the air, as it drifted relentlessly downward.

Covering her.

Bringing darkness.

Shea came. The orgasm just rushed through her.

She was climaxing as he began to thrust.

For the first time ever, the darkness called to her, unleashing its own wicked pleasure. Excitement built up inside her again, close on the heels of the first.

Her skirt brushed against her cheek and nose. It fluttered against her face with every inhale she took. She couldn't see. All she could do was feel, and listen, and ohhh . . .

"Derek," she gasped.

His abs flexed against her butt as his cock worked in and out, burying himself deep. Her pussy grabbed him and held him tight.

"I—" Shea cried.

Derek's shout rang out, and then he was coming with her.

Pleasure rocked her. "I love you, too."

Sixteen

The Somnambulist was frantic. He needed to get to his beloved. He ached for her. Didn't she ache for him? His energy was so low, his particles were barely moving. Some had already drifted off. Bit by bit, he was detaching. Dying.

"She-a," he hissed. "She-a!"

He flew to the next window, peering inside. He shouldn't be here; he knew it. The mean Wreaker had almost gotten him last time he'd visited her. That had been nights and nights ago, but he was still out there somewhere. Dark eyes glowing, hot hands burning . . .

The creature winced. He still hurt. The spot where the Wreaker had touched was gone, unfillable. The pain had been unlike any he'd experienced before, too much to enjoy.

But he had to get to her; his She-a was in trouble.

The face in the window was back!

The Somnambulist floated outside her window, willing her to wake up. She didn't move. She slept on peacefully, ignoring him, oblivious to his panic. His particles reverberated in annoyance, humming so badly he almost lost a few more. He should leave. If the Wreaker wanted her so badly, *he* could save her.

But where was he?

Flying around the second story of her building, the Somnambulist double-checked the guest bedroom and the bathroom. The rooms were empty. Still, this might be a trick.

Bad trick, if it was. Dangerous.

He scampered back to She-a's window and pressed his particles flat. Concentrating, he tried to get into her head from a distance. "Open eyes. Listen!"

He screeched when his lovely rolled on the bed, away from him.

"No!" His particles swirled, and he spun around in midair. The moon suddenly caught his eye, and fear filled him. Dark clouds floated over the glowing crescent. "Painted sky. Good time to die."

His particles shook until they were keening. What was he supposed to do? He couldn't leave her like this, not his beloved. Not his one true soul mate.

Down below, a flick lit the darkness. The creature gasped when he saw oranges and yellows and reds. Fire! The evil human had brought fire!

Anger made the colors dance inside his head. He couldn't let it happen again, his beautiful girl could never stand it. With a scream, he dive-bombed the intruder.

Out of control, he tried to push the figure in black away. His particles just skimmed around the solid body. Wildly, he tried to penetrate the waking entity and take it over. None of it helped; his powers only worked in the land of sleep.

The oranges and yellows and reds got brighter, building like his temper . . . Twisting like his fear . . .

Barreling upward, the Somnambulist tumbled into She-a's room, sprawling at the foot of her bed. The move nearly splattered him apart. Gathering himself together, he crawled up onto the mattress with her. Not going slow like he was supposed to, he shoved his essence into her.

She moaned and her body curled, her knees pulling into her chest.

"Sorry, sorry," he said, already unfurling her long legs and putting her feet on the floor. "We go walk now. Tonight we *run*."

He moved too fast, not situated inside her correctly, and her body lurched sideways, almost falling down. The Somnambulist growled, pulling her upright and pushing her toward the door at the same time. The footboard of the bed dug into the side of her leg. Pain shot through them both, nice and juicy.

He gobbled it up, letting the power help them both.

"Open door," he huffed. "Run down stairs. Skip down stairs. Fall down stairs."

He didn't care how; she had to move!

Down the stairs she went, tripping once. The creature clung to the railing with her hand, stopping her from tumbling all the way down. "One step, two step. Please, my pretty!"

Finally, they made it to the first floor. The creature's

nose scrunched. He could smell the bitterness in the air, feel the awful tickle in his beloved's throat.

"Flat floor. Easy now. Go fast."

He pushed, yanked, and shoved her to the kitchen.

"Look," he panted. "Look. See the face—"

Pain suddenly ripped through him like a hot, electric knife. It cut through him. . . . Cut him off from her . . .

The creature screamed as he was wrenched backward. He twisted as the burn sizzled and scorched him. It was too much, excruciating. He tried to get away, but couldn't.

And he knew what that meant.

Reaching out with every cell in his being, he clung to She-a instead. Without her, he wouldn't survive. She whimpered and stumbled back.

"Shea!" a dark voice rumbled.

The Somnambulist lurched, coiled, and struggled. The pull was unbearable. Too much pain. It hurt. It hurt.

He held on tighter, the molecules of his toenails digging in. She-a screamed, and his palms turned slippery. Tears rolled down her cheeks. He tried to stretch out, but was caught inside her. He tried to disperse, but couldn't. In this form, he was stuck.

Then, with an agonizing heave, he was suddenly out of her.

Out of his home . . . Away from his playmate . . . Without his love . . . He reached for her, wanting her. *Needing her.* "She-a!"

"Her name is *Shea*."

Looking up through pain-filled eyes, the Somnambulist saw a tough, dark gaze.

He saw his death.

Shea was dreaming in a world that looked like her own but was somehow heavier. The shadows were deeper, the air more sultry. Even the feel of her skin was more erotic.

The sound of a scuffle made her turn and her breath caught when she saw Derek tangling in her living room with . . . with . . . a thing? A creature?

She couldn't take her eyes from it. It was tall and wispy. She could practically see right through it, but as Derek's hand wrapped around its bony shoulder, she could make out a definite form. It had long, spindly legs with knobby knees. Its fingers and toes were abnormally long, but its chest was small and sunken in. The face, though, captured her. Mostly snout, it was one of those faces that was so ugly, it was almost cute. Almost . . .

But its eyes . . .

Her heart squeezed.

Its eyes were unbearably lovely. They were soft as they held her gaze adoringly, longingly . . .

"Derek," she whispered. She couldn't stand to see it in pain. Couldn't take—

"Look," the creature whined, ignoring its captor and the pain it was obviously in. Derek's hand moved toward its forehead, but it squirmed away. Concentrating only on her, it pointed one bony finger over her shoulder. "The face. *The face in the window.*"

Shea turned.

When she transitioned from sleep to wakefulness, she didn't know. Yet suddenly, she found herself alone in her kitchen with tears on her cheeks.

And somebody was staring in the window right at her.

Her scream lodged in her throat. Fear froze her.

The stare down was silent and shocking—until clouds drifted away from the moon. In the dim light, Shea saw a wisp. A malicious, snakelike wisp curled upward from her watcher's hand.

Her fear morphed into fury, and she charged toward the sliding glass door. "You bitch!"

"The face in the window."

Derek's head snapped up, and two realizations hit him simultaneously. Shea could see them, and someone was outside.

Oh, God—her stalker! His head snapped from the window to the Somnambulist and back again. What was he supposed to do? He couldn't deal with them both at once, not even split as he was.

"You bitch!" Shea yelled, bringing his attention back fast.

She was awake and alert—and moving so fast toward the sliding glass door it scared him. He took a step to stop her before he remembered he was in Dream Wreaker form.

And he had a wiry, nasty Somnambulist to deal with.

He turned to take the thing out fast. With all its particles bunched so tightly, it was at its most vulnerable.
He reached for the creature's forehead but it squirmed
away, seemingly triple-jointed.

"Help her," the thing whined. "Let *me* help her."

"She can't stand any more of your help," Derek
snapped. "She wants you gone."

"Liar!" The Somnambulist writhed like an eel, trying
to get away from the burning touch at its shoulder. It
saw the hand coming at his forehead, and it ducked. "I
help her. She needs me. She always has."

"You scare her."

"I protect her."

Derek looked worriedly toward the sliding glass
door but he couldn't see what was happening. He had
to get back to his car, where his body was sleeping. He'd
moved farther away from her to lure the Somnambulist
in, but he hadn't expected *this*. He had to get out there
and help—

A screech pierced the air outside. "You . . . you crazy
maniac!"

"She-a!" The Somnambulist bucked, nearly throwing him off.

Derek grabbed on with both hands and smelled the
thing charring.

Still, it struggled, its eyes on the doorway. "Let me
go. I showed it to her. Where were you?"

That jab hit too close to home. Unable to help himself, Derek gave the thing a shake. "Is that why you came
back? Is that why you're here?"

"She's mine," the thing hissed, its eyes turning beady. Pain contorted its mouth. "We've been together forever and ever."

"She's mine," Derek growled.

Using his weight, he pinned the thing down. It was stronger than it looked. It had taken more power from her than it should.

Enraged, he leaned down closer. "You make her do things she doesn't want to do. You take her places she doesn't want to go. *I saw you touch her.*"

The thing actually stilled. "She-a touches, not me. We're a team. Soul mates."

"Shut up!" Derek reached for its forehead again, but roared when the thing bit him.

His grip loosened, but instead of dispersing, the creature started crawling toward the sliding glass door. "My pretty girl. My beloved."

Derek caught it by its ankle. Flipping it on its back, he overpowered it.

The Somnambulist's eyes looked up at him, sad and heart wrenching. "Painted sky. Time to die."

Its puny chest heaved up and down.

"Don't let She-a die, Wreaker. You're mean, but don't you let her die!"

In its own way, the thing did love her. But Derek was a Dream Wreaker, and he had a job to do. Even if he scared this thing off Shea, it would just take on another host. As mature as it was—and as sexually aware as it was becoming—he couldn't let that happen. He'd seen fear in his lover's eyes one too many times.

He cupped his palm over the creature's forehead.

It whimpered and caught the place on his forearm where it had bit him. Instead of pushing him away, though, the Somnambulist pulled him closer. "She can't hear me; she doesn't listen. You have to tell her. . . . Promise me you'll tell her. . . ."

At first Derek thought it was another trick. When he saw the yearning in the thing's eyes, though, he leaned down.

The creature whispered into his ear, and the words had him pulling up fast, his heart racing. He looked into the thing's onyx eyes. It wasn't lying.

"Let her know I loved her."

All Derek could do was nod.

Then he made it fast and clean.

Merciful.

And the Somnambulist was no more.

Exploding out of the sliding glass door, Shea found herself face-to-face with the person who had been terrorizing her—the woman who had been breaking into her home, messing with her things, and toying with her mind.

"Lynette!"

Caught in the empty backyard, the woman froze. "Stay away from me," she hissed. "I'm warning you."

Light suddenly caught the corner of Shea's eye, and her head snapped toward the window. Her breath seized. A fire burned on the windowsill where Lynette had been standing, curling and dancing in the darkness.

Instinctively, Shea stepped back. It was then that she spotted the newspaper. Crumpled newspaper was packed in wherever it would stay, in the nooks of her kitchen window and at the base of the building under the aluminum siding. Worse yet, expired matches lay on the ground.

"You . . . you crazy maniac!"

Shea rushed forward and knocked the burning paper onto the ground. Spinning around, she clenched her fists tight. "What's wrong with you?"

The anger on Lynette's face deepened to rage. "I'm *not* crazy," she hissed. "I know what you are."

A metal can came flying at Shea and hit her in the side, splattering liquid all over her Mets jersey night-shirt. She flinched at the unexpected sting, but it was the scent of lighter fluid that had her pulling up short.

Astonishment came over her as surely as horror.

This wasn't just some sick mind trick; Lynette was trying to kill her. "You're out of your mind!"

"Me? You're the one who's possessed. I've seen it in you!" Lynette was desperately trying to light another match.

Footsteps suddenly pounded behind her.

"Shea!" Derek yelled.

The match hissed against the starter strip, and a flame sprang to life. Watching her defiantly, Lynette tossed it toward the newspaper she'd bunched up on the ground. The tiny flame danced atop the tip of the match, then caught. It licked its way quickly across the paper, doubling in size, tripling in an instant.

Shea stiffened, terrified beyond measure.

And incensed beyond thought.

With a fierce growl, she charged forward. If Lynette thought she'd go for the fire first, she was wrong. Shea's fist flew out, her full weight behind it. Her knuckles met Lynette's chin, and the woman went down hard, yelping.

The sound turned into a scream when Lynette fell onto the burning newspaper.

Fire quickly ate its way up her sleeve. Spatters of the lighter fluid fed it, making it more voracious. Shea watched in horror as flames exploded across the black sweatshirt.

Lynette's scream ripped through the night.

"Shea!" Suddenly, Derek was there, pulling her out of the way. "You've got starter fluid on you. Stay back."

She struggled in his arms. "Roll," she yelled at Lynette. "Put it out."

Her would-be arsonist just sat there screaming and slapping at the fire that was quickly nearing her shoulder.

All the terror and fright of that night so long ago built up in Shea's chest. She couldn't watch this happen again. When Derek ran to get the garden hose, she hurried back to Lynette. Taking care not to get too close, she shoved her bare foot against the woman's hip. "*Roll*, Lynette. Drop and roll!"

The woman finally got the message. Flopping like an oxygen-starved fish, she ground her shoulder into the grass. She sputtered when a stream of water hit her full-on.

"You crazy, fucking bitch." Derek doused their assailant thoroughly. "Shea, are you okay?"

"I'm . . . I'm fine."

"Are you sure?" he barked.

She looked around. No flames leapt into the night sky. Nothing popped or snapped. Smoke still trailed upward, but she could smell fresh air. "I'm okay."

People started to appear out of doorways and leaning out of windows. Her next-door neighbor took over on hose duty, and Derek strode back to her fast.

"Why?" Shea rounded on her attacker. When she got no answer, she dropped down to a crouch to look into Lynette's face. "What did I ever do to you?"

"I have to stop you. You poisoned her. You're poisoning everybody!" Lynette wiped her wet face, then reached to cradle her arm.

Shea's brow furrowed. "Poisoned who? What are you talking about?"

"She was fine until she saw you interviewed on TV. By then it was too late. Your evil potions and creams had sunk into her pores. She couldn't get them off, no matter how many times she washed."

"I don't understand, Lynette," Shea said.

A fire truck had arrived, but Lynette shoved away the medic who was trying to look at the burns on her arm. The pain flared, and she doubled over. When he tried to help, she kicked at him instead.

"She knew what you did as a child. She'd seen how evil controlled you." Lynette tucked her legs underneath her and tried to get to her feet. The grass was slick, though, and she went back down. "She tried to ward you off then, but you came back."

Another whimper left the woman's lips, and she leaned over her arm. Shea looked at it, so red and bright, and her stomach turned. She knew better than most what fire could do to human skin. She reached out. "Here, let me see that."

Lynette lurched back. "Stay away from me."

"I can help."

"No!" Reaching into her pocket, Lynette pulled out a piece of bread—the Gypsy talisman against evil spirits. "Be gone, demon child!"

Shea froze. Everything stopped in that moment. Even the wailing of the sirens faded into the background. "Mrs. Lupescu?"

"The stepmother," Derek said, stepping closer.

Shea swallowed hard. "Is your stepmother Lorna Lupescu?"

"Fromm. Her name is Fromm!"

Shea folded her hands over her face. Oh, dear God!

"I saw it with you just now," Lynette hissed. "That Somnambulist was inside you. You've kept it with you all this time. You harbor evil; you're its tool!"

The fireman pulled back, a strange look on his face.

Shea cleared her throat. "Derek, would you get my briefcase?"

He looked at her, his eyes narrowing.

"Please? I'll be all right."

Shea sat back on her heels, her arms wrapped around

her knees. She'd done so much to separate her past from her present, but her past wouldn't stay suppressed.

She pressed her lips together hard. She and Lynette had been fighting the same battle. They'd both been trying to get rid of the parasite inside her, only Lynette hadn't cared if she'd taken Shea down with it.

Shea's fingers bit into her knees. She'd *seen* the thing with Derek. After all these years, she'd finally come face-to-face with it.

She winced when Derek came back outside and hit the switch for the exterior light. The bulb was bright, and her eyes struggled to adjust.

It was only then that she realized more firefighting equipment had arrived, as had the police. Officials were checking the building, making sure the fire was completely out and talking to witnesses. The fireman who was trying to treat Lynette finally managed to cut off the remains of her sleeve.

Derek's gaze met hers as he approached. Shea couldn't believe she was going to do this.

"Thank you," she said, taking the case.

Her hands shook. Adrenaline was still pumping through her veins. She took a deep breath and focused. Opening her briefcase, she looked for what she needed. "Do you give me permission to treat that burn?"

"What? No!" Lynette pulled back and hugged her arm to her chest. "Keep your evil potions away from me."

"You know it will help." Shea spoke with a calm she didn't feel. "You've got a degree in chemistry, and you read my lab book."

Lynette's mouth flattened even as tears coursed down her face. The skin on her arm was fiery red. The pain had to be hot.

Shea picked out two vials. "This is a silver ion solution that has antimicrobial, pro-healing, and anti-inflammatory properties for burn wounds. It's not evil. I won't hurt you."

"You're trying to trick me." Lynette looked away. The throbbing in her arm was so intense, she was rocking back and forth. "Make her go away," she said to the fire-man. "She's trying to kill me."

The fireman pushed his helmet back on his head. The look he shot Shea was sympathetic.

"I should inform you it doesn't yet have FDA approval." When Shea still didn't get a response, she closed her eyes. She wasn't dealing with a sane mind. "It's the antidote, Lynette."

"What?" Her secretary's head snapped back, and her eyes narrowed.

Shea pushed away all her feelings: her shock, her resentment, her outrage, and her hurt. "You're right," she whispered. "A Somnambulist has been possessing me all these years. He's made me do evil things, but this is the antidote to all that lotion my company has been selling. If you'll agree not to tell anyone about me, I'll give it to you."

"Liar!" Lynette hissed. Still, there was a look of hope in her eyes.

Derek dropped down onto his haunches beside her. "Mind giving me some of that stuff, Curie? I singed my fingers a bit back there."

His fingers were perfectly fine. Still, Shea nodded and concentrated on measuring out the correct amounts and mixing the active ingredients.

"You're a bigger person than I am," Derek said softly.

Shea glanced toward Lynette. "I hate that the first person I'm helping is the one who tried to burn down my home."

He looked down at the solution in her hands. "That's quite the advancement, Curie."

She swallowed hard. "The wrinkle cream was just an interesting side product. This was what I've been working toward ever since I got my PhD."

He gave her a soft smile. "You're going to help so many people. Your dad's going to be so proud." Leaning closer, Derek wrapped an arm around her shoulder and kissed her temple. For a moment, she pressed her face into the crook of his neck.

Then gathering herself, she finished the preparatory work she'd done so many times in the lab. She dabbed a bit onto Derek's knuckles. He flexed his fingers and stood.

She looked to Lynette.

The woman's mouth worked.

"Fine," Shea said, turning away.

"Give it to me!" Lynette looked ready to cry.

Shea handed the finished product to the fireman. "An occlusive dressing works best, but treat the burn with this first. Sorry, it's a bit messy."

She watched as he did first aid.

Her goal was to aid those who suffered worse burns, those unfortunate victims who now ended up scarred and in pain. She hadn't yet figured out the best delivery method for the treatment, but she was working on it. If only something like this had been available the night of the trailer fire . . .

She blinked, tears coming to her eyes. That was just too much to think about right now.

She focused on putting everything away, but by the time she was done, her whole body was trembling. She pushed herself to her feet and instinctively turned into Derek's arms. He gathered her up close and moved them back into the shadows, away from the crowd.

"She's out of her mind," Shea whispered. It was only hitting her now what had happened, what *could* have happened. . . . She pressed her face against his chest. "She didn't even think of the other people in the building."

She heard his heart beating under her ear. It was racing fast, just like hers. They both knew the woman had been intent on just one target. "I should have made the connection," he said.

"How?" Shea's fingers dug into the muscles of his back. His cheek was pressed against the top of her head; his embrace was tight and secure, protective. "I never knew what happened to Mrs. Lupescu after we moved away."

"I should have spent more time on the background search."

"You were looking into Lynette's background, not her stepmother's."

"It doesn't matter. I should have been the one to stop her." His fingers tangled in her hair. "I was sleeping in my car. It took me forever to get here."

"No, *I* needed to stop her." She'd been fighting against the unseeable for so long. "I just didn't mean to hurt her."

"She meant to hurt you." Derek's voice turned hard. "It was self-defense—and one hell of a punch, by the way."

"When you grow up as the possessed freak of the North Solstice Trailer Park, you learn to defend yourself."

They both looked at the woman sitting and rocking back and forth on the ground.

"She's been watching me sleepwalk," Shea whispered. "She knew the Somnambulist was back."

Derek rubbed her back gently. "It's over, baby. It's really over."

Shea glanced up at him uncertainly. "All of it?"

The night fell silent. Somewhere nearby, a cricket chirped.

"You saw it, didn't you?"

Shea nodded. She'd only been in his world for seconds, but she knew all the stories were true. Dream Wreakers. Somnambulists. . . .

Her heart squeezed. Those soft, loving eyes. God, she didn't want to ask. "Is it . . . gone?"

A muscle in his jaw tightened. "It won't be bothering you anymore. *Neither* of them will be bothering you anymore."

"But . . . how will we ever know what really happened?" She watched as the fireman finished up Lynette's dressing. "How will we figure out who did what? Or why?"

"It doesn't matter." Derek hooked a finger under her chin and looked into her eyes. "All I care about is that I've got you to myself, safe and whole."

She sighed. "We're really alone."

"Yes, Curie. It's finally just the two of us." His eyes darkened. "And you won't believe how I'm going to take advantage of that tonight."

Seventeen

T his is all my fault."

Shea looked at Phillip sharply. He was sprawled in a chair in her living room, arms hanging limply off the sides. At Derek's insistence, she'd stayed home from work. She hadn't realized that would make everyone at Biodermatics even more concerned. Phillip and Tamika had shown up on her doorstep not long ago.

Phillip, in particular, was not handling things well.

"How can you say that?" she asked. "You were attacked just the same as me. Worse, in fact. Lynette confessed to it when she was questioned."

"Yes, but you had concerns about hiring her. I was in too much of a hurry to listen." He looked at his shoes morosely. "Next time I question your woman's intuition, just slap me upside the head."

Everyone stared at him.

That shook him out of his gloomy mood a bit. Reaching up, he ran his fingers through his hair. "Well, maybe you could make that a gentle nudge."

"Or maybe you should just put me in charge of hiring the office staff," Tamika said.

She crossed her legs, and her foot bumped the coffee table, which was laden with cards, candy, flowers, and even a teddy bear. Well-wishers and curious neighbors had been dropping by all day.

"Now that's an idea," Phillip said, sounding serious.

Shea snuggled into the corner of the couch and tucked her legs underneath her. She was glad her friends had come. The quicker things got back to normal, the better she would feel.

"If we're taking blame, my name needs to go on the list."

Shea looked over her shoulder toward the kitchen. Derek stood in the doorway, looking tough and fit—and thoroughly pissed off with himself.

"I should have dug deeper into that two-year break in Lynette's work history."

Shea dropped her arm onto the back of the couch. "But she did take a break to care for Lorna."

"Whose problems were psychological." He clapped his hand against the doorjamb. "I should have caught that."

Phillip leaned his head back against the chair cushions. "Derek, medical records are sealed."

"Thank goodness," Shea muttered. She certainly didn't want anyone poking around in *her* medical history.

Leaning down, Derek opened the bag of Baby Ruths that Tamika had brought over as a get well gift and went back to the kitchen for drinks. Shea drifted her fingers across his hand as he walked by.

"You guys know how guilty I feel when I eat those things," she said. Still, she couldn't take her eyes off the tempting chocolate. "If my dad caught me, he'd change my name and never take me to a Mets game again."

"We won't tell. Besides, you need to celebrate. You could have died last night." Tamika opened a candy bar. "I always knew the woman was weird, but I never thought she was certifiable."

Shea suppressed a shudder. "She was the primary caregiver for Mrs. Lupescu for a long time."

Derek set down glasses of milk and squeezed her shoulder.

"After a while, sanity must have blurred with superstition," he said quietly.

Phillip glanced uncomfortably toward the backyard. "Bruce showed me that production schedule. She was trying to shut us down any way she could."

Derek stared at a burnt spot in the backyard, and Shea watched him closely. His face was emotionless, but his fingers were stiff against her shoulder. He held a lot in sometimes, but there were signs of the emotions going on under the surface. Signs that she was beginning to understand he only let her see.

"We'd changed the locks on the doors, and that threw her," Derek said. "When she wasn't able to get inside, she had to improvise. The lighter fluid came from the next-door neighbor's barbecue."

Shea cleared her throat uncomfortably. "Can we all agree that none of this is our fault?"

"I'm all for that," Tamika seconded.

She crossed her legs and Shea winced when she saw the zebra stripes.

Sometime shoes were just shoes.

"I didn't like her from the start," her assistant said matter-of-factly.

"Really?" Phillip grinned. "We couldn't tell."

Derek looked at Tamika. "Why have you stopped running?"

She hesitated for a moment. "I haven't stopped. I've just been too busy to train regularly."

"Doing what?" Shea asked. "Why all the late nights?"

Tamika's eyebrows rose. "Has somebody been watching me, too?"

"Come on, Mika," Phillip said dryly. "You've got to admit you've been a little testy."

Their assistant's gaze met all their looks. "Have I really been that bad?"

Shea shrugged.

"I'm sorry. I've just been tired." Tamika slumped back against the cushions. "I didn't want to tell you yet, but I've been going to night school."

Shea blinked. "But that's great!"

"I might have loaded up too heavily on classes."

Phillip sat forward. "What are you taking?"

"Business management." She played with the fringe

on the pillow tucked up against her side. "I didn't like it when you hired that twit in at the same level as me. I know she had a background in chemistry, but I've been working at that job for three years. I'm *good* at it. Biodermatics is going places, and I want to be a part of that. I know I can do more. I want to be office manager."

Shea reached out and caught her friend's hand. "I think that's a great idea. You should have let us know—we might be able to work out a more flexible schedule for you."

"Or help with buying books or part of the tuition," Phillip offered.

"Really?" Tamika looked surprised and more than a little touched. "That would be fantastic."

"You deserve it." Shea could have kicked herself for not coming up with the idea on her own. "I'm sorry we've taken you for granted."

"No more of that," Phillip agreed. He rose from his chair. "Why don't we go grab a cup of coffee and talk about it?"

Tamika's speculative look swept over Shea and Derek. "Yeah, I think it's time we left these two alone."

Shea blushed, but wrapped her arms around her friend's shoulders when she leaned over to give her a hug.

"I'm so happy you're all right," Tamika whispered. She gave Derek's hand a squeeze, too. "Both of you."

Shea lifted her cheek for Phillip's kiss, then Derek escorted their guests to the door. When he closed it and turned, that purposeful look was back in his eyes.

Shea let out a long breath. She loved the way he looked at her.

He started to cross the room. "I thought they'd never leave."

She stretched out more fully on the sofa. Eyelids heavy, she lay back against the armrest. When he crawled up over her, her hands went naturally to his waist. He kissed her neck and settled his weight on her.

"Feel better?" His lips brushed against the lobe of her ear.

"Mmm. Those loose threads were bothering me. I'm glad we know everything now."

He tensed and pulled up slightly.

"What is it?" she asked.

His hand came up to cup her face. Slowly, his thumb caressed her cheek. "Actually, there's one more thing I have to tell you. Your Somnambulist shared something with me before he . . . left."

Shea's chest squeezed. "Do I really want to hear this?"

"You do. It's about the fire when you were twelve."

Goose bumps popped up on her skin, and a shiver ran down her spine. Shea stiffened. "I don't—"

"You *didn't*."

She stilled.

"You didn't set the fire. Neither did your Somnambulist."

Breathing was suddenly difficult. "I don't understand. How can you be sure?"

"It was an electrical fire. The wall went snap, crackle, pop."

"What?"

"That's what the Somnie said. Sparks came out of an outlet in your bedroom. You were sleeping and didn't realize what was happening."

Her fingers bit into his waist. "But *it* did?"

Derek closed his eyes and dropped his forehead against hers. "It got you out of that fire, Shea. It wasn't your fault. Somnambulists aren't good for much, but that thing got you out of there."

Her breath caught. "It took me down the stairs to show me what Lynette was doing, too."

"It was trying to look out for you. It was . . . fond of you."

Tears suddenly pressed at her eyes. "What did we do, Derek? Look at how we repaid it!"

He shook his head firmly. "It had lived a full life for a Somnambulist. It was ready to go. It knew it was time to give your nights back to you."

The band of tension around Shea's ribs loosened, and then disappeared entirely. *He* was the one giving her nights back to her. Her nights, her days, her self-confidence, and her love.

She wanted to give him something in return, and she knew what he wanted most.

"Will you sleep with me tonight, my Oneiros?"

The darkness in his eyes intensified, and he went still.

She smiled up at him. They hadn't slept all night, and he'd waited such a long time.

"Sleep," she whispered. Gently, she stroked her hands along his lower back. "All night long, in my bed and at my side. Will you watch over me from the dream realm?"

With a groan, he leaned down and kissed her.

"Curie, I thought you'd never ask."